OTHER BOOKS BY

Donna Jo Napoli

SPINNERS

Spinners

DONNA JO NAPOLI & RICHARD TCHEN

DUTTON
CHILDREN'S
BOOKS
NEW YORK

Library of Congress Cataloging-in-Publication Data
Napoli, Donna Jo, date.
Spinners / by Donna Jo Napoli and Richard Tchen.—1st ed.
p.   cm.
Summary: Elaborates on the events recounted in the
fairy tale, "Rumpelstiltskin," in which a strange little man helps a
miller's daughter spin straw into gold for the king on the condition
that she will give him her first-born child.
ISBN 0-525-46065-9 (hardcover)
[1. Fairy tales.   2. Fathers and daughters—Fiction.
3. Spinning—Fiction.]   I. Tchen, Richard.   II. Title.
PZ8.N127Sp   1999   [Fic]—dc21   98-54640   CIP   AC

Published in the United States by Dutton Children's Books,
a division of Penguin Putnam Books for Young Readers
345 Hudson Street, New York, New York 10014
http://www.penguinputnam.com/yreaders/index.htm

DESIGNED BY AMY BERNIKER
Printed in USA   First Edition
3 5 7 9 10 8 6 4

WE DEDICATE THIS STORY
TO DOUG WEISS AND SALLY HESS

FOR help with so many kinds of spinning, we thank
Carol Bier, Barry Furrow, Eva Furrow, Nick Furrow,
Thomas Klein, Sandy Lin, Catherine Maule, Noëlle
Paffett-Lugassy, Ramneek Pooni, Dominic Sagolla,
Stephanie Strassel, Carol Woolford, and, last but not least,
Libby and Rudy Amann, who demonstrated spinning
and patiently tried to teach us how to spin.
For amazing fortitude, persistence, and insight, we thank
our wonderful editor, Lucia Monfried.

Young Love

One

LATE afternoon heat strokes the young man's belly. He watches the tiny beings in the air. Here in the hay and straw loft, there are more than he has ever seen before. And now he knows: They are angels, angels come to celebrate his love. The angels dance, and the young man, agog, lets out a long sigh of joy.

The young woman snuggles against him in her sleep. She is more beautiful than ever. He has trouble believing his good fortune. He has adored her for as long as he can remember. And now, finally, she reciprocates.

The first time they made love, she became perfect before his very eyes. This time, the second time, she is ethereal. If his eyes were sharp enough to make out the infinitesimally small air angels, he is very sure that they would be no more lovely than the young woman.

He rolls over, then, slowly slowly lowers himself onto her,

like the heaviest of blankets. He moves with such gradualness, she does not wake. He weaves his fingers through her fanned-out hair. Such beautiful hair. If any hair is golden, hers is. If any woman is precious as gold, she is. The simple necklace of shells that he gave her looks like the jewels of a princess against her mother-of-pearl skin. He brushes her cheek with his own.

Her eyelids flutter. She opens them and smiles. "Is it time already, my love?" She untangles his fingers gently and works her way out from under him. She stands, naked, statuesque, her back to him. The waning sunlight gilds the downy hair on her arms and calves. She turns her head quickly and looks at him out of the corner of her eye. She pivots her whole body, so he can admire. Then she stoops and kisses his forehead.

He pulls her onto him. "Don't go."

She laughs. "I have to." Then she grows serious, her pink lips rounding. "Are you nervous?"

"Of course." He releases her.

She rises and steps into her shift, tying it at the waist with a yellow sash. "Don't delay. Father knows I love you. He expects your request."

"But he made you no assurances." He dresses, as well. He takes a deep breath. He is a small man, almost exactly the height of the young woman. He buries his face in her hair, and straw rasps against his cheek. He steps back and picks the straw from her hair.

She turns to him with anxious eyes. "Check me carefully, please."

He examines her for straw. Then nods.

The young woman peeks out the triangular window that gives a view of the farmhouse and the road out front. Then she climbs down the ladder of the loft, runs across the barn floor, and disappears out the doors. The spotted cat, the only one disturbed by the young woman's motions, wanders to another patch of sunlight and curls up again.

The young man considers going out the back door, but it's too easily viewed from the farmhouse. So he follows the young woman, halting inside the big barn doors. She has left one slightly ajar. He moves to it quietly. He must protect the secrecy of his encounters with the young woman at least until her father agrees to the match and the amount of the dowry is set. He sticks his head out first, then walks quickly around the corner of the barn. He will cross the field and duck into the woods.

"Tailor!" The call is a demand.

The young man stops and faces the farmer. "Afternoon."

The farmer rests a hoe over one shoulder. He is tall, husky, strong. He walks over, more puzzled than suspicious. Or maybe the young man just hopes that it is puzzlement. "What's a tailor doing in my barn?"

"I slept in the loft." The young man had not planned his words, but as he speaks he realizes that sticking as close to the truth as he can is his best bet. He does not know how much the farmer has seen, but he knows the farmer is no one's fool. A bit of straw clings to his shirt. He picks it off carefully, as if to prove his words.

The farmer drops his head forward a little. "You slept in the middle of the afternoon?"

The young man runs his hand down his neck, trying to

calm his jumpy flesh. Tailors work by day, especially on days when the sunlight is bright like today; he needs an excuse for his aberrance. He scratches at his back, made prickly by the straw. "I love the smell of the hay, the cushion of the straw under me." These are truths, though odd ones. Most people want a layer of cloth between their bodies and the straw. But the young man likes to hear the little crush noises as he rolls, he likes the tough hollow canes that hold cool air in summer and hot air in winter.

The farmer scratches at his own shoulder as though the young man's itchiness is contagious. "How much do you like it?" And now his face is, perhaps, shrewd. "I'll sell you straw. A whole roomful if you want. I need the hay, for feed. But there's an excess of straw."

The young man listens carefully to the music of the farmer's voice, to the rises and falls that should tell him if the farmer is asking for pay in exchange for his silence. But today the young man's ear is deaf to the nuances. He cannot risk not buying the straw.

They settle on a price, and the farmer agrees to deliver the straw the next day.

When the young man arrives home, a flat, square package wrapped in brown paper and tied with string sits on his front step. This is the deep brown cloth he ordered to make the burgher's new fall trousers. He puts the package inside, content. He is a weaver himself, as well as an excellent tailor. But he wanted a cloth more refined than he could weave for this special purpose.

Still he is proud of his own weaving, and especially of his tailoring. With hard work and luck, he and the young woman can make the life they want. She is a spinster, and a reasonably good one. She will shear and spin. He will weave and sew. They will be a team.

He washes and puts on his good shirt, good pants, his only pair of shoes. He runs his fingers through his clean hair. No mirror graces his home, but he knows he looks presentable. He has even features—nothing too stark, nothing too small.

It's time to address the young woman's father.

"A tailor has little to offer." The young woman's father sits on the bench at the eating table. The dinner dishes were cleared hours ago, but he prefers to talk at a table. His elbows anchor themselves on the dark wood.

"I already have a home. She will never be hungry. She will always be loved."

The heavyset man grinds his teeth in thought, his jaw muscles rippling visibly through his skin. And for the first time, the young man is truly afraid that her father might say no. He must have the young woman. He has already bought the ring: the thinnest strand of gold circles once around the finger, then swirls in and out to make a round knot on top. He spent most of his savings on it, and he carries it with him everywhere in a pouch that hangs from his neck. He has already planned the marriage bed he will build for them—large and sturdy and comfortable. And the new stool for her spinning wheel. The list goes on. But now, oh, now her father ruminates too long.

The young man must move the matter forward. He clears his throat. "About the dowry . . ."

"Dowry? You want me to pay you for taking such a prize? It should be the reverse. My daughter is worth more than you will ever make."

That is true. But if the young man gives in too easily, they may revert to the question of whether or not there will be a marriage at all. "It is customary . . ."

"The miller asks no dowry, and he insures her a better future than you ever could."

"The miller?" The young man feels as though he has received a blow in the middle of his chest. "That old man?"

The young woman's father nods. "He's had his eye on her for years."

"But your daughter loves me." The young man leans forward, his breath comes hard. "Please, sir, you know that."

"So she says. Still, the foundation of marriage calls for more than love."

"And I offer more than love." The young man rises to his feet. "I'm a tailor; she's a spinster. We work well together. We can make a good life together."

But the older man is shaking his head. "Anyone with a needle and a good eye can be a tailor. But this town has only two mills. The miller will always have more business than you."

"Excuse me, sir, but if she were to marry the miller, she'd spend half her life as a widow. Your daughter and I are young. We'll save up and buy sheep. We'll grow our own fleece for yarn. And with me she will have children."

"Old men can father children."

"He goes out drinking every night."

"Maybe he won't, once she's at home waiting for him."

"Please, consider: With me, she will have happiness."
The young man comes around the table and drops on one
knee. "She will be radiant, like gold."

The young woman's father looks unhappy. "Gold. The
miller said he'll cover my daughter with gold. And he can do
it, too."

That braggart. The young man's blood heats. "I know
how to treat your daughter. I'll treat her good as gold."

The young woman's father laughs. "You poor tailor."

"If you give me her hand in marriage, I will dress her in
gold." The words blurt from the young man's mouth. The instant they are out, he wishes he could pull them back.

The young woman's father laughs again. "What nonsense."

"It's not nonsense." The blood pounds in the young
man's ears. "A gold wedding dress. You'll see."

The young woman's father frowns. "You have the means
to make her a gold wedding dress?"

The young man nods, though he has no idea where he
will find the means.

"Are there things about you I don't know?"

The young man nods again, for it is true. Her father does
not know that the young man has already consummated his
marriage with the young woman.

"All right, then. If you make her a gold wedding dress by
the time of the next full moon, you may marry her. If not,
she will wed the miller."

Two

H O W could you promise that?" The young woman's fists are on her hips. Her face is at once angry and sad. "Where will you get the money? Look!" She sweeps her arm across the room. "You've spent what little money you did have on filling this place with straw!"

The young man catches her hands and pulls them together. He kisses them. "It wasn't enough money to buy gold cloth, anyway, my sweet."

"You're saying crazy things. You're doing crazy things."

"And you are here, in my home. That's crazy. You've never entered here alone before. People will talk."

She pulls her hands back and shakes her head in confusion.

"Maybe people should talk." He speaks slowly, as the idea comes to him. "Maybe if you're disgraced, your father will see that I must marry you. Besides, you're old enough to claim the right to your own choice."

"How can you say such a thing?" Her brows furrow. "I want to marry the right way. My mother would have wished that for me, may she rest in peace." She crosses herself. "I want to marry with his blessings." She puts both hands on his shoulders and looks him in the eye. "You must find cloth woven from gold yarn, my love. I can't marry the miller, that shaggy bear of a man. You must make me a gold wedding dress. You made the boast—now you must make good on it somehow. Find a way. Fast. Please, please. My sweet love, please."

For a week the young man racks his brain, but to no avail. He broaches the subject of a loan with his brother, but his brother turns his empty palms up; he has recently been sick and is down on his luck himself. And the young man cannot earn enough to buy the necessary gold cloth in less than a year, but the moon grows fuller every day.

He overcomes his distaste for the miller's loud ways and surrenders his pride: He goes to the miller's house. But once he gets there, he realizes the futility. He doesn't knock.

The young man stands beside the mill until evening falls, watching the wheel go round. He takes the wedding ring out of the pouch and looks at the gold knot on top. His eyes go from that gold knot, like gold yarn, to that huge wheel. This wheel secures the miller's life. Would that the tailor had such a wheel.

But the only kind of wheel the tailor knows is a spinning wheel. And all a spinning wheel offers is yarn and thread.

That's all he needs, though. Thread. He could spin his own gold thread.

He walks the road slowly, the sound of the miller's wheel growing fainter. He could borrow the young woman's spinning wheel, for it is low and can spin any kind of fiber. But no. He will not ask her. He does not want her to know what he has come to.

And now he thinks of the old woman whose yarns he has often bought. All the other spinners the young man knows live with their husbands, and husbands are unlikely to let them lend their wheels. This old woman lives alone, like the tailor will if he doesn't get a spinning wheel. Her spinning wheel is low, like the young woman's. He can borrow her wheel, and she will be grateful for the break from work.

He runs, the certainty of what he must do drying his tongue. The night air pricks at him, like hundreds of tiny needles. He is parched by the time he reaches town. The fountain in the market square burbles softly. He drinks deep of the blue-black water, then winds his way through the footpaths between the city homes.

The old woman's home is small and old, but well tended. She stands in the doorway, as though she waits for someone.

"Good evening, madam."

The woman lifts her face. The milky film over her eyes shines wet in the dusk. "Tailor? What brings you here at this hour?"

"A favor. I've come to borrow your spinning wheel."

"My wheel?"

"Just for a week at most. A welcome pause in your toil." He speaks quickly, practically stumbling over his words.

"I never lend my wheel."

"It will be an exchange, of course. I'll mend your clothing."

"I mend my own clothes."

The tailor imagines the nearly blind old woman fumbling with a needle. He grinds his teeth in frustration. "I'll mend your curtains, your coverlets." His voice rises with fervor. "A fair exchange, madam."

"Tailor, you've always been a fine customer, and your business is welcome. But I won't lend my wheel. Let a poor woman be." She turns and goes inside.

The young man is astonished. His request is simple—her refusal, incomprehensible. He follows her. "I'll mend everything. I'll make you new dresses."

"Hush, young tailor. You're almost out of breath." She sits on the only chair in the room, situated in front of the spinning wheel.

The more the young man looks at the wheel, the more he covets it. "I must have it."

"I could never lend it."

The tailor falls to his knees, as he knelt before the young woman's father a few days ago. "Sell it to me, then."

"It's not for sale."

"I'll pay anything."

"You sound like a desperate soul." The old woman shakes her head.

"I need this wheel."

"No other wheel would let these blind eyes spin. Find another."

He picks up the wheel.

"Don't dare take it without my blessing."

"You leave me no choice. I'll return it when I've finished." If he spins gold yarn, he'll have the blessings of the young woman's father—that shall have to be enough.

. . .

The young man stands in the room filled with straw. He rubs his hand along the clear, smooth wood of the spinning wheel. The old woman's wheel is the finest low wheel he has ever seen. He hadn't realized that before tonight. Indeed, it had seemed quite ordinary—but now he can see it is anything but.

He takes a handful of straw. Other plants yield yarns—there's no reason why straw can't yield a yarn that shines golden to the eye. And if it has the sheen of gold, isn't it gold yarn? Isn't it, isn't it? Oh, God, please.

He spins.

The straw breaks.

He spins.

The straw cuts his drying skin.

He licks away the blood and spins.

Bits of straw fly into his eyes, up his nose, down his throat.

He coughs and spins. "Please, wheel. Please."

The next handful of straw holds together against the wheel. It forms a strand. Oh, mercy, a gold strand. The young man goes to twist it around a spindle. It breaks.

Brittle yarn. Unweavable.

The young man is lost.

But he cannot simply give up and watch the miller take his love.

He grabs another handful of straw and spins.

The young man does not leave the room. He does not eat. He does not drink. A day passes. Another.

He spins. "Please. I am your supplicant. Please, wheel."

And, yes, the spinning wheel whispers. It maddens the young man. His foot moves automatically on the pedal now. His hands flail. He is tired and hungry and crazed. Only half the straw remains intact. The rest he has broken to useless dust. He screams and gets up from the spinning wheel. He throws himself into the straw and cries. He would give anything for gold yarn.

When he rises again, the damp straw beneath him smells oddly, as of the sea. He stumbles to his feet. Moonglow lights the room, gives the straw a sheen. The young man grabs a handful: simple straw. Yet he is certain of the gold within.

He takes this tear-wet straw and spins, despite his aching back and hands and eyes. His right leg cramps painfully, but he pedals harder and faster and harder and faster.

By dawn, he has a skein of gold yarn. It is straw, his mind tells him. Yet it holds firm and supple like gold. Divine gold. He stares.

He spins the rest of the straw; then his hands fall to his lap.

But his leg pedals. The wheel spins. He tries to hold his leg still, but it pedals. He presses on it with both hands. It pedals. He throws himself backward until he lies on the floor, away from the spinning wheel, which comes to a halt. But his leg still pedals away at the air. It pedals all day. It pedals all evening. In the moonlight, the shadow of his leg looks like a monster fighting a phantom, endlessly, relentlessly. He falls asleep pedaling the air.

The next morning his body lies quiet. He sits up slowly, groggily. Then he remembers. He looks quickly at the spinning wheel; the gold filament dazzles in the sunlight. He did not dream it. His hand goes to his mouth in awe.

But this is not a moment for hesitation. The yarn must be stretched out on a loom; it must be woven into cloth. He will weave the cloth for the young woman's gown by himself, for it would be impossible to find a skilled enough weaver willing to drop everything and make the cloth fast. And he needs the cloth fast. It will be full moon soon, too soon.

And there is another reason he doesn't want to hire a weaver: He does not trust the gold filament in anyone's hands but his own.

His stomach growls. He laughs. He will boil a whole chicken and gnaw the skeleton clean, then crack the bones and suck out the marrow.

He stands and falls. That leg that pedaled at the air all yesterday, that leg stays bent. He massages it. He works till the sweat forms on his forehead and chest and belly. But the leg remains bent like a bird wing.

He shouts. No one comes.

He gets up. Balancing on his good leg, he hops to the window. From outside come the clucks of his neighbor's chickens. He could never catch one now, not with his leg contorted. He will have to wait till the cramp goes away.

He hops out the door to the well, stumbling twice on the way. He drinks from the well water. Then he hops into the neighbor's chicken coop. If the neighbor sees him, she will come to his aid. She will not begrudge him what he takes now. After all, he made the dress her youngest wore to her confirmation.

He reaches into a nest and grabs an egg. He cracks it into

his mouth and swallows it whole. He eats another. And another. And another.

He hops back into his house, leaving the front door open as an invitation to anyone who passes.

He rubs his loom with a dry cloth, then arranges the yarn. The treadle is different from the spinning wheel's pedal. It requires pressing only after each pass with the shuttle, to lift the wooden harnesses. His crippled leg can manage that. He weaves the gold yarn all day, his nerves clacking with the loud clack of the harnesses. No one enters the open door, though he can hear wagons pass on the road. He weaves till evening. He pauses for more water, more eggs. Then he weaves into the night. The next day he weaves, pausing only for water, eggs. He weaves until every bit of yarn is used. It is a long piece of cloth, and wide. It will suffice.

He rolls himself in it and sleeps soundly on the floor.

"Ah! My love, it's beautiful."

The young man opens his eyes.

The young woman strokes the gold cloth that has come loose from him during the night. She drapes it around her middle, her shoulders, and up across her head like a shawl. Her smile glistens no less than the gold cloth. "You did it. You bought gold thread. You . . ." She sees him now. Her face goes horror-stricken. "What has happened?" She runs to him, kneeling in the gold cloth. She picks straw spikes from his hair. "Raw egg crusts on your chin, and your cheeks are hollow, and, my love, what has happened to you?"

He smiles. He must look a sight. "I will make you the loveliest gown ever." The dust in the air dances around her head like a halo. There are so many dust angels now, all borne of the straw. "No one ever will be more glorious than you."

She sits back on her heels. "It is truly beautiful. I love it. How did you find the money for it?"

"I spun it. Myself."

"You mean you wove it."

"Yes, but I spun it, too."

"From what?"

He opens his hands to the air. "Can you see?"

"What? I see an empty room."

"Exactly. Before, there was straw."

"Straw?" Her eyes widen. "Gold yarn came from straw?"

He rises on one foot. The foot of his bad leg now slightly curls under and toward his other leg.

She stands, as well, her face pinched in confusion. But now she looks at his leg. "What's wrong with you?"

"A cramp. Will you help me massage it?"

"Of course. Lie back."

They work together, rubbing, pressing, rubbing, pressing. He watches the concentration on her face. She seems to welcome the job. He understands: The task holds fear at bay. He rubs and presses, rubs and presses, his diligent hands almost wearing the skin from the flesh.

Three

THE young woman rubs the young man's leg as he measures the gold cloth. She leaves for chores, then comes back and rubs his leg as he cuts the gold cloth. She rubs and rubs.

The young man's leg curls under him. He leans on her for support just to get from one side of his room to the other.

"How did this happen?" she asks again, her voice thinning in a whine of frustration.

"I spun too many hours without pause."

She blinks the tears from her eyes. "You scare me when you talk of spinning straw into gold." She snatches a scrap of cloth from the floor. "Watch." She bites it. "This is real gold cloth. Teeth don't lie." She whispers, "This didn't come from straw."

"Massage. Please."

Her shoulders cave slightly. "I'll return tomorrow." She

goes to kiss him, hesitates, then turns on her heel, out the door. She's back a moment later with a cloth wet from the well. She scrubs at his face.

"You washed me yesterday, my love. I'm clean."

"But there's something wrong." She scrubs harder.

He grabs her by the wrist. "What's wrong?"

"I don't know. You don't look like you."

He forces a laugh. "I'm me. I'm your future husband."

Her free hand moves to her throat. She stares at him, as though trying to see inside him. Then she gives him a quick kiss. "I'll be back tomorrow." She wrests herself away and leaves.

The young man pets the gold cloth. He patiently sews, starting with the bodice. He takes the smallest stitches possible so the dress will be strong. After all, they will dance at their wedding.

He looks at his curled leg.

Perhaps ten more days till the full moon. No cramp lasts ten days.

He sleeps poorly that night, despite his exhaustion.

"Open your eyes and drink."

He jerks awake.

The young woman kneels beside his bedroll. A sweet, sickly smell rises with the steam from the mug in her hand.

"What is it?"

"The midwife helped me mix a brew against cramping. Chamomile with the yellow St. John's wort flower and so many other things." The young woman smiles, but only the corners of her mouth lift—her eyes are flat. "Drink."

"Maybe the cramp is gone already." The young man sits

up and looks at his foot. If anything, the curl is tighter. He drinks.

She is already kneading his calf, pulling on his toes. All day long, she comes and goes, fitting massages between her chores. All day long, the tailor sews.

That night he sleeps even worse.

The next day, she brings another brew. The taste is more bitter. Another day passes.

The night twists and turns. At one point he comes fully awake, only to realize his leg is pedaling the air again. He pins it under his healthy leg and stares at the ceiling.

By midmorning, the young woman is trying on the dress. He adjusts the darts, the length of the sleeves, the oval of the neck. She talks of how surprised her father will be. Her voice is light with false gaiety. They do not speak of the morning brew, of the daily massages. They do not look at the curling leg. It seems the young woman doesn't even look at the young man's face anymore.

He sews. She gathers remedies.

Finally the dress is finished but for hems on the skirt, wrists, collar. The young woman stands in the center of the room, her gown brilliant. She clasps her hands. Her close-lipped smile doesn't hide her worry; rather, it accentuates it. "You can't walk down an aisle. You can't even walk alone."

His cheeks sag with lack of sleep. "I've been thinking about that. Your father demanded that I make you a gold wedding dress by the next full moon. But he didn't say the wedding had to follow right away. Tomorrow is the full moon. I will show him this gown. Then we can set a date. For a few months from now."

"A few months?"

"My leg will be perfect by then." His voice quavers. "Three months. Four. Maybe five at most."

One hand goes to her mouth. She rushes outdoors.

The tailor hops on his good foot after her.

She is stooped over, heaving.

"Have you been tasting my awful brews?"

She wipes the vomit from her bottom lip and looks at him in silence.

"Watch out; you'll dirty the dress. Come in and change."

She gives a little laugh. "Yes, keep the dress clean." She walks inside and changes into her shift. "I can't wait a few months."

He takes her in his arms. "I can't wait either. But we don't have to wait for anything except the wedding itself. We can be together here, make love here. Once we're betrothed, we can set up our business together. We'll say we spend the day with you spinning and me weaving. No one will bother us."

She pulls away. "I must wed soon." Her eyes move from his feet up to his face. They are full of fear.

The next morning the brew is accompanied by a hot poultice. The massages are harder, longer. Her panicked fingers leave white marks on his flesh.

By twilight the hem is complete on both inner skirts and the huge outer skirt. The gown is worthy of a queen. The tailor folds it carefully and wraps it in brown paper. He ties the bundle to his back. With the help of a walking stick, he hurries to the house of the young woman.

Her father awaits him. "You're hobbling, tailor."

"I've brought something." The young man lifts the package from his back.

"What's the matter with you? You look sick."

"Here."

The older man's eyes fasten on the package. He unwraps it with eager hands. And now he's fingering the folds. He pulls his candle closer and holds the cloth to his eye. "My daughter was right: It is gold."

"Let us talk of a wedding."

The father tilts his head. Worry lines his face. "You're leaning on a stick."

"It's a cramp from spinning, nothing more."

The older man frowns. He peers at the tailor's face. "You're sallow. The bags under your eyes could cradle a newborn."

"I haven't had much time for sleep."

"You're diseased, tailor." The man's voice grows loud with conviction. "Better that my daughter should marry the old miller than a diseased tailor who isn't long for this world."

"It's the candlelight that makes me look so poor."

"Is that so?" His voice is doubtful, yet not totally harsh. "Sleep tonight. Come again tomorrow, tailor. Come in full daylight on two strong legs, and we'll set a date." The young woman's father pats the gold cloth. "You can leave the gown."

"I'll keep it till we set a date."

On the long walk home, the tailor curses his leg. Would that the cramp be gone by tomorrow. He grips his vile walking stick tighter. He knows that from a distance he presents the figure of an old man. That's when he remembers the old woman. He never returned her spinning wheel, and it's been what? More than two weeks. He had promised to return it when he finished.

He'll hire a boy to carry it back to her tomorrow.

He thinks of her sitting at that spinning wheel, year after year, pedaling, pedaling. She knows all about spinning—all about spinners' ailments. The idea comes to him in a burst: If anyone knows how to cure this cramp, she will. She can't still be angry at him once he returns the wheel. She'll help him. Especially if he offers to pay. He changes his route.

By the time he arrives at her door, it is full night. Yet she stands in the doorway, like last time. "Good evening, old woman."

"Tailor? I thought I'd seen the last of you."

"I forgot because . . ."

"You forgot my livelihood?"

"I was busy and my leg . . ."

"What about your leg?"

"A cramp. I got it spinning on your wheel. How do I make it go away?"

She frowns. "It won't go away."

"What? How can you say that?"

"You have what you deserve."

"I don't deserve this. All I did was borrow your wheel. I'll have it brought to you tomorrow."

"I don't believe you."

"Here. Look at this." The young man takes off the bundle.

She carries it inside and unwraps the gown. "You made this?"

"Yes. You can keep it till tomorrow, till I have your wheel returned to you."

"All right."

"And then you can help me cure this leg."

"We'll see about that."

He hobbles home and falls onto his bedroll. He lies on his back, his hands working the muscles of his crippled calf and foot, hour after hour after hour.

He wakes to late morning in a pool of sweat. The hottest part of summer is not yet here, but the air is already heavy and thick. Where is the young woman? He has come to expect waking to her smelly brews and strange poultices. He lies on his bedroll, drifting in and out of sleep.

Finally hunger forces him to rise. He eats.

The young woman comes in. "How's your leg?"

He tucks it under him.

She sits beside him.

"You weren't here this morning." He can't keep the accusation out of his voice.

She turns to the young man and takes his hands. "Your leg's getting worse."

"It's temporary."

"You don't know that. It's been half a month."

"Wait," he says. "You'll see. A few months at most."

"I don't have time to wait."

"Why not?"

She looks down, and a hot tear drops on his hand. "I'm marrying the miller."

"Don't be crazy." He pulls her toward him. She pulls away. "You hate the miller. He's an ugly old braggart."

"It was your boasting about being able to dress me in gold that started this whole mess."

"I did what I said I'd do. Your father and I made an agreement."

"But look at your leg."

"This won't last, I tell you. And even if it does, I'm still the same. I can still sew. I can still love. And, oh, my sweet, I can spin straw into gold. We can be rich." He kisses her hands. "Look at me."

"I can't bear to look at you." She cries openly now. "I can't stand to hear you rave about spinning straw into gold. I can't abide your dreadful leg."

"Don't say that. I'll be strong and straight again soon. Wait for me."

"I can't." She leaves.

Four

THE young woman rubs her huge belly. She stands at the edge of the garden by the mill, her husband's mill, now her mill, and appears to be staring at the mill wheel.

She does not know that she is watched, in turn.

And no one but the young woman and the watcher know that the child within is not the miller's.

The child is due any day now. The woman spends much time indoors. On those rare occasions when she comes outside, she seems to drag her feet. The watcher wishes he could massage those feet. He remembers when she massaged his foot.

Winter is coming to a close; the new leaves are the size of mouse ears; the birds chatter.

The young man would steal away now, but he cannot go anywhere quietly these days. He hobbles on one foot with the help of a cane. His cramped leg withers day by day.

The stand of pines close to her home offers him protection now, as it has since August. He watches.

He is still a tailor, and he has more customers than before, out of generosity for the afflicted. But people are not more friendly than before. Indeed, no one talks to him more than to exchange a quick greeting or to arrange business details.

The young man is lonely. But he keeps himself busy. In addition to sewing, he now spins. With his good leg, naturally. It is as though he has a gruesome obsession with the act. And, after all, he has a fine spinning wheel.

The boy he eventually hired to carry the wheel back to the old woman reported on his return—wheel still in his arms—that she wanted nothing more to do with the wheel or his leg. He never found out what became of the gold wedding gown.

So the young man spins, and the whole time he spins, his crippled leg pedals the air as though working an imaginary wheel of its own. When he stops spinning, his good leg rests, but the crippled leg wavers for a while. He no longer tries to stop it.

And he weaves these days, too. He enjoys the rude clacking of the harnesses when he presses the treadle. The noise is as nasty as his dreams.

This is his life.

So the only important thing that has changed, really, is that the young woman doesn't love him. And that is everything.

He wouldn't have expected a young woman to shackle herself to a cripple. Especially with a baby on the way.

He blows hot on his hands. They are big. Bigger than expected for a man of his small stature. He could hold a baby safe, cupped in those palms.

Oh, to cup those palms around the young woman's roundness.

She walks past the mill and into the miller's house.

The young man hobbles home. He despises the miller. He does not envy a larger home, fields, a mill. He envies only the privilege of living with the young woman.

"Psst. Sir. Psst." The boy leans in the open window.

The young man's bedroll stretches out immediately under that window. He sits up, half asleep. "Where is she?"

"In her garden."

The young man reaches in the dark for the small money pouch hanging from his belt. He hands the boy a coin.

The boy leaves.

The young man is already mostly dressed. He puts on a light cloak and one shoe. The toes of his curled foot have twisted so now that foot cannot fit in the other shoe—but that is no matter, for it barely touches the ground. He has sewn it a kind of mitten for warmth. He hurries along the road in his jumpity way. He knows the young woman would not be out in her garden before dawn if there were not some special reason. The right time to give the ring that still hides in his pouch has come at last.

He has an agreement with the boy, who sleeps and works in the mill. Whenever the young woman leaves her home, the boy is to notify the young man. The boy thrives on this arrangement. His legs are already plumper from the extra food he buys with the coins. The young man does not thrive. Knowing where the young woman is, knowing her every move, eats away at him. Yet not knowing would be worse.

A crow screams as it takes to the air. He almost stepped on it. He feels uneasy, as though the crow is a bad omen. He doesn't like birds that eat carrion.

The sun peeks the slightest bit over the horizon. He looks into the eye of the sun and knows: This will be the day his child is born. The hairs of his neck bristle eerily.

He hurries.

The woman stands in the dry, empty winter garden. His heart beats to the bursting point. He comes directly to her. And he is shocked. They once stood about the same height. Now his contortion brings his head only to her nose. And he seems to have lost half his weight while she seems to have doubled hers. Still, as the dawn sun hits her hair, she lights up spectacularly. Her hair glitters gold. And, oh, the angels dance about her head still. He pulls the ring from his pouch and holds it out to her.

She gives a sad smile and closes her fist around the ring.

His heart goes aflame with joy. She loves him still. He'll take her back. Generosity warms him everywhere.

"You walk with a stick," she says. Tears roll down her round cheeks. "You poor ugly man."

His eyes sting with unexpected fury. "Ugly? Is that what drove you away? I thought you were afraid I couldn't provide."

She blinks, taken aback. "I did worry."

"Well, you were wrong. I have more business than ever."

"And I'm glad for you," she says quickly.

"Yet you call me ugly."

She swallows her tears. "I'm sorry I said that. I only meant that you're so . . . so rumpled. I shouldn't have said that."

"You said you loved me."

"I did love you. I brought brews and poultices. I argued with my father. I prayed, but your leg didn't straighten."

"You know nothing of love. You share the miller's bed yet I'm sure you don't love him. You love no one."

"Don't be cruel." She sobs. "I'm so sorry. But it's true: You are no longer my love."

"And who are you? What will the miller call you when he sees my son crawl from your womb?"

She wraps her arms protectively around her belly; her eyes instantly glitter with fear. "This is not your child."

"You know it is."

She lifts her chin defiantly. "Before this moment, I felt sorry for you. But as you spoke, your features crumpled in upon themselves. Your soul is as rumpled as your body." She tosses her hair back. She narrows her eyes. "What do you want? I will pay what you ask."

He cannot answer.

She turns to go.

He grabs for her and falls.

She stops, looks down at him. "Pathetic wretch. You diminish us both." And she names him, a new name, a name of revulsion.

He notices her ankles; they puff out over her shoes. He thought before that his own heart would burst, but now he thinks that she will burst, as well.

She leaves.

The young man gets up with difficulty. Mucus runs down his shirt. He cannot stop crying.

What has brought such unbearable punishment? All he did was spin straw into gold. And for naught, for he still lost the young woman.

That afternoon labor begins. The boy tells the young man, who goes as quickly as he can manage to the mill. From his hiding place, he sees the midwife enter; he watches the boy carry buckets of water. He thinks he hears noises from within the miller's house, but maybe it is just his own insides rolling within his skin.

He will wait for the baby's cry. Then he will enter and declare his fatherhood. The baby will resemble him. Whatever the miller looks like underneath that thick beard, he will know the child can't be his own. He will throw out the young woman, and she will turn to the young man.

He wipes away the liquid that runs into his eye. He looks at his hand. It is covered in blood. He has been digging his finger into his forehead, digging to the rhythm of his hopes. He wipes his hand on his trousers and leans against the tree.

Night falls. There is commotion inside the miller's house. The boy races off and returns with a second midwife and the priest. The priest! The miller throws open a shutter. The young woman's screams fill the air.

The screams stop. A newborn cries out and a woman wails. The miller staggers out the front door, walks across his field, aimless.

The boy comes out with an empty bucket.

The young man hails him. "What has happened?"

"She died."

"Who—the baby?"

"No, the lady."

The young man falls to his knees.

The miller has a daughter. He'll raise her. She'll love him. The tailor will be no one to her.

The tailor straps the spinning wheel to his back. He doesn't say good-bye to anyone. What would be the point? No one cares where he goes or what he does. Not even himself.

He walks the road south out of town.

PART TWO

Survival

Five

SASKIA skips along the road. The morning sun glistens off the dew on the black-eyed Susans, and the wrens flit in joyful mating dances, and, yes, the whole world is wonderful wonderful.

"Wait up, please," calls Dagmar.

Saskia circles back to her friend, skipping higher and higher. She would take flight if she could. "Your brothers always disappear somewhere around here."

Dagmar nods. "They have a secret path."

"Do you know it? Do you know where they go?"

"Yes."

"Then let's go there."

Dagmar slows to a walk now, still breathing heavily. "It's far from the road, and we'd be alone. I don't want to do anything to make the miller whip me."

"My father would never whip you." Saskia's shock makes her voice brittle.

"Yes, he would. He protects you like some jewel in an iron box."

Saskia holds her tongue. By day, Father is the successful miller. By night, he is a noisy drunk, full of boasts and threats. Everyone knows this. Father has his own still—a natural side business for a miller. An entire cellar is devoted to his jugs of gin. But for all his noise, he never harms anyone. "I want to go. It's an adventure. And if Father finds out, I'll tell him I insisted."

Dagmar considers Saskia. Then, with sudden conviction, she marches ahead. Within a few moments, they intersect a path and turn onto it. The path soon opens onto the lake. Dagmar weaves in and out of the trees at the water's edge, then points. A thick rope hangs from a willow branch. Another hangs from the next tree over. And the next. Ropes hang from all the trees.

"My brothers swing from tree to tree," says Dagmar.

Saskia spins around, imagining the boys flying past. She laughs.

"They swing over the lake and jump in."

Saskia is already pulling off her shift. She stands, arms soft by her sides. With the utmost care, she lifts the shell necklace over her head and places it safely on her shift. This was her mother's necklace. And the ring she wears on her thumb—the one with the fluffy gold bird's nest—was her mother's ring. The midwife who delivered Saskia gave her these treasures for her birthday this spring. She said her mother's last request was that Saskia should have them when she turned ten. Saskia straightens each shell on the string—they are all there, all fifteen. She touches the shell ribs fondly, pulls off the ring, and sets it in the largest shell—she always turns the necklace so that the largest shell hangs in the very middle.

She climbs up to the lowest branch of a willow and swings. Her blood rushes with the air. The water shimmers below, too far below. She keeps hold of the rope and swings back to the branch.

Dagmar is beside her now, her tummy termite white. "I'll show you." She swings out over the lake, flies free, and splashes.

"Tell me when." Saskia swings, eyes squeezed closed.

"Now!" shouts Dagmar.

With a scream, Saskia plunges into the cold water. Her whole body tingles.

They pass the morning swimming. Then Dagmar sits in the sun drying, while Saskia swings from tree to tree. Eventually, Dagmar rises and puts on her shift. "I have to help shear the sheep."

Saskia puts on her ring, her necklace, her shift.

"You're strong." Dagmar pats her hair in place. "And you're pretty." She turns and walks back to the path.

Saskia wants to return the compliment, but Dagmar is plain. "You're adventuresome."

"Ha. Is that the best you can offer?" Dagmar walks more quickly. "Your mother must have been beautiful. The miller is so ugly."

Saskia never saw her mother. Mother died in childbirth. But everyone has told her how very beautiful Mother was. The words about Father hurt, though. "Father's not ugly."

"Of course he is, Saski. The miller is ugly as sin, with those bleary eyes and wild hair."

"That's just messy."

"It's all the same. Why do you think he's never married again? No one will have him."

Saskia walks in silence several minutes. "Dagmar, I need your help."

"What?"

Saskia's cheeks go hot. She has wondered why Father never took another wife. She has always told herself that Father must have loved Mother so much that no other woman could touch his heart. But maybe that was wrong. "Tonight, when my father comes home from the inn, when he falls to the floor and passes out, you and I will cut his hair and shave him clean."

"What! Not me."

"He sleeps like a dead man, Dagmar. I promise you. When I was little, I used to try to wake him to get him to climb into bed. But I never could. He won't catch us; he won't even wake."

Dagmar is still shaking her head. "Shaving is easy. You can do it yourself."

"But that's just the point. For you, it's easy. You help your mother groom your brothers. But I've never held a razor. Please, Dagmar."

"My father would beat me if the miller got mad at me. What if the miller refused to mill our grain? The only other miller is far on the north side of town."

"I bet Father will like how he looks afterward. But if he doesn't, I promise I won't tell him you helped." Saskia hooks her arm through Dagmar's as they come out of the woods and cross the grasses to the road again. "Please, Dagmar."

Dagmar moves her mouth silently. Saskia knows she's

chewing on the inside of her cheek. Dagmar does that when she's worried.

"I can't ask anyone else. You're my best friend, Dagmar."

Dagmar looks at Saskia and nods. "I'll do it."

Dagmar and Saskia whisper, hiding now in Saskia's room, waiting for the miller.

The front door opens with a loud clank. The miller's heavy footfalls cross the floor. The girls hear a thump on wood. And now nothing.

Saskia goes into the common room. Father is asleep in the chair, his head on the table, his breath heavy with berry schnapps. Maybe he's been with Marcus; Marcus grows berries and supplies Father with them. Daniel supplies him with pears. Rufus supplies him with peaches. Friends come and go with the breath of each month.

Saskia lights the hearth fire to heat the pot of water that already hangs there. She sets a lit candle on the table.

While the water heats, she and Dagmar attack Father's hair. Saskia holds up a lock; Dagmar shears it off. They do one whole side of Father's head. His ear emerges, smelly and grimy. Saskia breathes as shallowly as she can. Now she holds his beard, and Dagmar cuts close to the skin. One side of his face is ready, finally, for the shave. Saskia takes the warm water from the fire. She dips in the cube of soap, rubs her palms together, and gently lathers Father's rough moustache and beard.

The razor flashes silver in the candlelight. Dagmar puts one hand on Father's temple and presses. With the other hand, she brings the razor to his cheek. Saskia gasps as the blade touches. And now there is a patch of skin, whitest skin, with splotches and small craters. The patch grows as the blade follows the line of Father's cheekbone, of his jawbone. It is as though the blade strips Father—makes him almost obscene. Saskia shuts her eyes.

"Help me," whispers Dagmar.

They lift his head and turn it so the other cheek rests on the table. They start all over again. Within the hour, Father is shorn and shaved.

Dagmar holds the candle close to Father's face. Saskia stares. Father's nose seems larger without that hair beneath it. His chin seems smaller. His lips seem fuller. He is familiar, yet unrecognizable. And he is altogether ugly.

Dagmar makes a scoop of her nightshift, and Saskia fills it with the shears, the razor, and the cut hairs. Dagmar blows out the candle. "He'll look better by daylight," she whispers.

Saskia doesn't trust her voice not to crack. She mumbles, "Mmm. Thank you."

Dagmar kisses her cheek and leaves.

Saskia smothers the hearth fire, dumps the water out the window, and goes to bed. She stares up into the dark. Dagmar was right: Saskia must look like Mother—for she looks nothing at all like the miller.

She turns on her side. On her tummy. On her back once more. She rises and returns to the common room. Father's snores come at regular intervals. Saskia lights the candle again and looks thoughtfully at Father. If his hair were cut a bit more evenly, that might improve his looks. She takes the meat knife. Holding the tips of his hair with one hand, she cuts with the other. But the knife catches, yanking the hair.

Father's eyes open. He jerks his head back, and the knife cuts his cheek. "Ahi!" He mumbles incoherently before his head drops with a clunk onto the table.

Saskia finds a cloth and presses it to the knife cut. She cries softly.

Six

GRETCHEN stands at the door

with one hand above her eyes to shade out the sun. "Saskia, come," she calls for the third time.

Saskia watches out of the corner of her eye. She digs the hoe blade into the ground. This is their herb garden; by summer it will be thick with chives and sage and marjoram, enough spices to last them all year. The dirt turns over in cool, damp clumps. Earthworms wriggle free.

"Don't make me have to come out in that dirt and bring you in myself."

Saskia wipes at the itch on her nose with the back of her hand. Gretchen couldn't drag her in. Gretchen is old and sickly. She wheezes when she moves too fast. But she has taken care of Saskia since she was a baby. Saskia owes Gretchen obedience. She twists, and with her heel she knocks a clod of earth from the hoe. She leans it against the side of the house, then brushes off her hands.

"He's asking for you, Saskia. He won't get out of bed."

Saskia sighs. Father has done this for as long as she can remember—climb into bed in a pique of anger and not get out for a week.

"He's got his back turned to the door and his shirt over his head." Gretchen lowers her voice. "He can be so ornery."

Saskia stiffens in distaste. She feels disloyal talking about Father behind his back. She walks to Father's room. "Good morning, Father."

"Daughter." Father throws off the shirt that lay on his head. He rolls to face her, keeping his body in a tight arc. His hands cover his cheeks. He lowers them slowly, pulling the flesh of his cheeks down. He buries his hands between his knees.

Gretchen gasps behind Saskia. "Your hair! It's all gone. And your cheek!" She rushes away.

Saskia steps forward gingerly. "I'm sorry, Father."

"Someone wanted to ridicule me."

Saskia kneels on the floor beside Father's bed. Her face is level with his. "No one wanted to ridicule you."

Gretchen comes in with a bowl of steaming water and a clean rag. She dabs at the knife wound on Father's cheek.

He lifts an arm to ward her off. "Can't you see it's clean?"

Gretchen purses her lips in argument. "Was it a brawl or a bet? Your brags will be the death of you, I swear. Who cut you?"

"I don't remember a thing."

Gretchen makes a *tsk*ing noise. "You have to remember a cut like that."

"I don't."

"Well, you must remember losing your hair. That's not something that happens every day."

"I remember nothing."

Saskia cannot believe her luck. But, then, that means Father thinks someone else shaved him and cut him—someone who wanted to ridicule him.

"It will grow back," says Gretchen softly. She twists the wet rag in her hand. Her face is full of pity. "I'll make you a hearty breakfast. That will cheer you up." She leaves.

Father grabs Saskia's wrist, just like he did last night. "I've been visited. Oh, daughter, I've been marked."

Saskia struggles with her silent tongue.

Father has been in bed a month. A whole month. This is longer than any of his past bouts. He leaves the room only in the middle of the night; Saskia hears him stumble outside and relieve himself. Gretchen brings him meals. Saskia brings him gin. Gretchen would scold her if she knew. Gretchen fights with Father about his drinking. Saskia wishes she could be like Gretchen; she doesn't want to bring Father the jug, but Father's threats frighten her.

People are angry at Father for not milling their grain. Dagmar's father has asked Saskia when the mill will run again. The two youths who work for Father threaten to seek employment elsewhere. They cannot afford to go without pay much longer. Gretchen grows sour and tense.

Saskia wants to confess that she cut Father. But Dagmar has made Saskia swear to secrecy. She is convinced secrecy protects them both.

The summer is almost over. Saskia stands in the huge

vegetable garden that she has fashioned from Father's untended wheat field. She picks green squash and stacks it in the wheelbarrow. It lines up neatly in rows on top of rows. Her arms are strong enough to push it, even full to the brim. The walk into town takes twice as long pushing the barrow, because she has to skirt carefully around the ruts. Still she has learned how to maneuver successfully and she rarely drops anything. She adds another row, so the pile stands high above the sides of the barrow.

As she wheels the barrow past the house, she listens outside Father's window. He snores his drunken snore. His head hair curls down his neck now and his face hair is already scraggly. But the tip of the scar from the knife still shows under his eye.

Father drinks by day as well as by night. There is no one to stop him now that Gretchen has left. Gin, always gin. Saskia longs for the old days, when Father still saw his friends, when she could tell the growing season by the smell of his schnapps.

It's all her fault.

But how long can it be her fault? He should cease already. She rolls the barrow to the road. Her feet pound the ground, giving rhythm to her guilt.

She moves faster, until she's almost running. Today is Wednesday, one of the best market days, for on Wednesday the king's mime troup performs in the center of the square. People who come to market only once a week come on Wednesday. Saskia will position her barrow away from the other vegetable vendors—near the flowers. That way the green of her squash will stand out. And the flowers will make the vegetables seem fragrant. Buyers will realize that a little squash added to a sauce makes it thicker.

The front wheel bounces in a rut. Squash fly.

Saskia stoops, gathers the vegetables.

"What's the hurry?"

Dagmar stands beside her, hands behind her back. Her round cheeks puff out in pleasure. She thrusts a hand forward, offering a muffin.

"Thank you!" Saskia bites in. The hot muffin bursts with raisins. "You made it, didn't you? Come teach me. Come this afternoon."

Dagmar laughs. "There's nothing to teach in muffins. They're not complicated like the things Rudolph makes."

Saskia thinks of the baker and his son, Rudolph, and the treats she used to buy from them. "Gretchen's been gone since the start of summer. I'm learning to cook and clean and do laundry."

Dagmar nods. "You were spoiled before. I envied you. But now you're so much worse off than me."

Saskia fights the rise in her chest. When the miller milled, they had money and they spent it. Now they have nothing. She eats quietly.

Dagmar moves her mouth, and Saskia knows she is chewing the inside of her cheek. "Mother says you have a lot of backbone, but no matter how hard you work, you'll be in trouble soon."

I'm in trouble now, thinks Saskia.

"She says the coming of fall will leave you hungry."

Saskia has been dreaming about fall. And winter. These dreams can be called nightmares.

A horse-drawn wagon rumbles by, loaded with baskets of pears and plums and peaches. Father has a wagon in the barn. But Saskia cannot use it, for Gretchen took their horse in payment for her last few months of work. Saskia looks covetously at the farmer's horse now. The farmer and his two sons wave.

Dagmar and Saskia wave back.

Dagmar clears her throat. "The miller's hair is almost long again. He'll look like a mountain sheep soon." She laughs nervously. "My father hasn't talked to the miller in a long time."

No one has, thinks Saskia. She takes up the handles of the barrow again. "I have to hurry if I want to sell all of these."

"Good luck. I'll come over this afternoon." Dagmar smiles. "I'll teach you how to make muffins."

Saskia shakes her head as if she's coming awake. "I don't know what I could have been thinking. We don't have any flour left."

"A miller without flour," says Dagmar softly. "I'll bring some. And raisins, too."

"No. We have plenty of squash. Squash makes a good muffin."

"You're crazy. The muffins will be green."

Saskia laughs. "Green's my favorite color." She pushes the barrow down the road.

The market teems. Saskia pushes her barrow past the row of dairy farmers' stalls. She thinks of their two remaining cows. If only she can keep them fed through fall and winter, maybe she can use their milk to keep soul and body together.

She knows how to make fresh cheese, at least. She used to help Gretchen do that. She'd never have enough cheese to set up business in the market. But maybe she could trade cheese for the other things she and Father will need.

Saskia parks her wheelbarrow in the middle of the flower tables and twirls the ring on her thumb round and round in worry.

Seven

THE spinner sits by the side of the road. His legs are folded under him; his chest rests on them; his forehead lies like a lump on the ground. He is half asleep. His hands move automatically to the rope that circles over his shoulders and under his arms—the rope that holds the spinning wheel to his back. It is secure. He closes his eyes. Dawn will come within the hour. He sleeps.

The sound of horse hooves wakes him. But he is practiced; he does not startle easily. He holds himself still as a dead man.

The horse comes close, whinneys, stomps.

"Let me get it, Father."

"Go on."

The child jumps to the ground. "It's not on a pile of junk. It's . . . it's on a man, Father!"

The spinner opens his eyes. He turns his head and looks

up at the boy and his father, who now stand over him, aghast. He keeps his face as calm as he can—he aims for a serene look. Oh, he has no self-delusion. He has seen himself in looking glasses. The slant of his body makes its mark even on his face, so that his left ear, left eye seem to rise. But with the correct mind-set, he can lessen this distortion. He makes all thoughts bland and looks steadily at the boy and man.

At the same time, he is conscious of the man's boots, of how an unplanned move can turn revulsion into fear, in the merest instant making those boots a formidable enemy. He readies himself for retreat back into the woods.

But the man's face holds no hostility as he leans forward. "Are you in need?"

The spinner rises to his feet, slowly, ever so slowly, to give the man and his son time to adjust to the sight of him. He straightens his clothes, brushing at his sturdy trousers, his fine sleeves. The whole time his eyes move slowly from the face of the man to the face of the boy and back again. He presses at the wrinkles in his right pant leg, which hide his curved, sticklike limb and make it seem as though the leg itself is as rumpled as cloth. It is the bane of his existence, that cursed leg. When he is as presentable as he can be, he lets his hands drop to his sides and waits.

The boy's mouth hangs open.

The man's mouth is closed in a tight line. His eyes are troubled. That could be a good sign. And his clothes are tattered, as are the clothes of the boy. Those are excellent signs.

The spinner swallows many times. He puts his hand to his throat to warm it. He wants his voice to come out wet and warm and mellow. "I spin better yarn than you've ever dreamed of. Your shirts will slip smooth on your back. Take me home with you. I can sleep in a corner." He doesn't say he can sleep in a barn or a shed, or, like last night, in an abandoned chicken coop. He hopes for a spot in their common room. "I'll give the woman of the house a break for a while." How long? Once he stayed in a place for two years before he tired of it. But usually he moves on in a matter of months.

"Ma's dead." The boy's face doesn't change; his eyes are wide and gray and unclouded. His attention is still on the spinner; his head is still full of wonder. His mother must have died long ago.

"All the more reason then." The spinner pulls his rumpled leg in toward his straight one and tries to look substantial. "If you have a loom, I'll weave, too. And I'll sew." He hesitates, then takes the chance. "You won't have to dress in rags anymore."

The man lowers his shoulders a little and pushes them back. He's a proud soul, after all. Still, he doesn't argue. The expression on his face is one of contemplation.

"It costs you next to nothing to offer me a corner," says the spinner in soft, reasoned tones. He holds out the hem of his own shirt.

The man feels the spinner's shirt between thumb and index finger. His eyes take in the weave of the cloth; they follow the cut of the sleeves. He looks at his son. The boy looks back.

The spinner is drawn to this silent pair. For ten years he has watched people from a distance—from a chair set aside from the fray, or a spot on the floor curled up by the fire, or even under the table. He knows how to interpret the shape their hands assume, the tension of their shoulders, the angle of their head. He knows that much of what is said is superfluous. This man and his son know that, too. The spinner feels the skin of his neck and chest slacken, as anxiety melts.

The man holds the horse by reins attached to a halter. So the horse obeys without a bit and bridle. The horse must be part of this quiet cooperation. The man slaps the center of the horse's back.

The boy jumps on. He reaches a hand down to the spinner.

The spinner takes the hand and pulls himself upward as the man hoists him from below. He throws his rumpled leg across the horse and nestles in behind the boy. His spinning wheel sticks out awkwardly past the horse's tail.

The man gets on in front.

The spinner puts the finishing touches on the collar of Thomas's jacket. Fall comes early this year. The boy will be wearing the jacket within the month.

He is alone in the small house, as usual. Thomas and Hansjakob are haying for a nearby farmer. They will come home exhausted when the sun sets. Then the three of them will cook together, eat together, and sleep all together in the single room of this home. The spinner has never been taken in by anyone so poor before. Yet he is more comfortable here than anywhere else he has been. He has exactly the same amenities as the boy and man—no matter that those amenities are few. He is treated as an equal.

And he earns his way. Thomas and Hansjakob wear new shirts and trousers, and there is an extra set in the chest under the window. The spinner now ties a knot in the thread and smoothes the front of the jacket. Indeed, with this jacket, the boy and his father have complete new outfits for winter, as well. There are tightly woven sheets on the beds—actually, on all three beds. The spinner allowed himself that indulgence, and Thomas and Hansjakob paid it no mind. There is one thick blanket completely finished and a second that is nearly three-quarters woven. The wool for the third is already spun. It is piled in neat skeins under the spinner's bed.

The spinner slowly folds the jacket into the chest under the window. A sadness weighs on his head, tugs at the skin of his cheeks. He climbs onto the chest, then drops himself out the window. He goes a short distance from the house and sits on the earth in the sun. It makes no sense to be sad, he reasons with himself. He has almost satisfied this small family's needs for a spinner, weaver, and tailor, but he doesn't need to fear that they will throw him out. He can spin yarn all winter, and they can sell it at market. He's done that before for many families. It's a suitable arrangement all around.

So there's no sense in being sad. He's been sad on and off for weeks now. And it makes no sense at all.

Plus today's a special day. It's Thomas's birthday. They will make a sweet bread tonight in celebration. The spinner has sewn the boy a kerchief to tie around his neck. He can wrap things in it for easy carrying. He can wipe the sweat from his brow with it. And he can cover his head from the sun or the wind or the rain. It's a good gift.

The kerchief is the first gift he's given anyone since he gave the ring to the young woman so many years ago. That was an impulsive and stupid act. She didn't even appreciate it. Thomas will appreciate the kerchief, though.

The spinner hops inside, but this time by way of the

door. His rumpled leg makes climbing up much harder than climbing down. He pushes the loom near the west window and sets to work on the second blanket. He weaves as the sun wanes.

Hansjakob and Thomas come through the door. The spinner didn't hear their approach. The farmer they hay for is so close, they don't bother to ride the horse there. And they talk so little, their voices don't betray them.

Thomas stands by the loom and puts his face close to the cloth in the darkening room. "Nice." His voice is full of appreciation.

The spinner warms under the praise.

They cook a dinner of green beans and pork fat and brown bread sweetened with prunes. They sit around the small table in contentment.

Hansjakob smiles at the boy. "Think it's time?"

"Yes, Father."

Hansjakob looks at the spinner. "Are you ready?"

"I am," says the spinner.

Hansjakob goes to his bed and lifts up the foot of the mattress. He takes out a slingshot and hands it to Thomas. This is no toy. The man cut the frame from hardwood, tempered it with fire, sanded it smooth.

Thomas laughs. "I'll kill us a rabbit tomorrow."

Hansjakob nods in approval.

The spinner goes to the chest and takes out the kerchief. He hands it to Thomas.

The boy rubs it against his cheeks. "Soft." He ties it around his neck and grins. "It's good to be ten."

Ten. Thomas is ten. For some reason the spinner never

questioned how old Thomas was. He's a thin, wiry boy, neither tall nor short. He could have been seven—he could have been twelve. The spinner has taken little interest in children since he became an itinerant. The children in the families he's worked for were shooed away from him by wary mothers.

Ten. The spinner's daughter is ten by now. Ten and a good many months.

"Now you have to plan a gift for my birthday," teases Hansjakob. "You can work on it straight from now till December. December eighth."

December eighth is Hansjakob's birthday. The spinner prepares to reveal that his birthday was two months ago. He never told the boy and man. He doesn't want them to feel guilty now about not having celebrated it. He should have told them. Maybe he'll lie. Maybe he'll say his birthday is in February. That would be a good time. He'll do that.

"Riga's birthday is next month," says Thomas. "I have to work on her present first."

The spinner perks up. He has never heard them talk of this Riga.

Hansjakob yawns and stretches his legs out straight. "We'll go visit."

"Good." Thomas comes around the table and hugs his father. "It's so far."

Far? The spinner squirms. He doesn't like traveling far. His leg pains when he can't stretch it often.

"We can stay for a week even, if you like, now that the spinner can watch everything for us." Hansjakob looks at the spinner for confirmation.

The spinner nods quickly and looks down.

Hansjakob clears the table and cleans up while Thomas goes outside for wood for the morning's fire. This is their routine. The spinner stays seated at the table.

All three of them go to bed early.

The spinner pulls his coverlet up to his chin. He pokes fun of himself inside his head. Here he thought he was treated equally. He had lulled himself into believing he was part of this family. How could he have fooled himself? For they are Thomas and Hansjakob, and he is still the spinner. Neither of them has ever asked his name. Maybe he has no real name anymore. Just the ugly made-up name that the young woman spat at him on the morning of her death.

But he does have a name. Everyone knew it when he was the tailor.

When he hears the regular breathing of the man and the boy, the spinner rises. He ties the spinning wheel onto his back. His every move is surreptitious. He walks down the night road.

Eight

THE ox-drawn wagon stops, and the spinner clambers down to the road. He turns to wave a thank-you to the smith, but the man faces forward; the wagon is already moving again.

The spinner picks a piece of meat from between his teeth and chews on it as he watches the wagon go. He doesn't really care that the smith didn't say good-bye. After all, what sort of a smith has an ox instead of a horse? And the spinner stayed with that smith only two nights. Just long enough to spin the right amount of wool for the smith's wife to make sweaters for their runny-nosed children. Not long enough to make a good-bye necessary.

The spinner secures the parcel of food that hangs from his belt. For the first time in a long, long while, he knows where he is going: back to the town he was born in, back to people who know him by name. Nevertheless, he has packed this food as a precaution; he dares not hope for a warm reception.

He takes the crossroad and walks as fast as he can, but that's still very slow. His spinning wheel grows heavier by the day. Plus his rumpled leg has suddenly turned more feeble; he leans on two walking sticks now, favoring his good leg so much that his back arcs toward it more each year. He feels old and decrepit, though he knows if he didn't have that rumpled leg, he'd be a strong man now, a man in the prime of life. A father carrying his third or fourth child on his shoulders instead of this infernal spinning wheel. He grips the walking sticks tight. He cannot afford self-pity.

That farm off to the right of the road seems familiar. It won't be long now till he sees the house he knows so well. Not long.

By midmorning he approaches his brother's house. He prepares to leave the road to go up the front walk when a child bursts out the door and runs into the yard. The child sees him, screams, and runs back inside. The spinner has never seen this child before. He stands in the street and waits.

His sister-in-law comes to the door. Her bosom has grown, as have her chin and her middle. The child he saw before peeks out from behind her skirt. Another smaller child peeks out, as well. The woman calls to him, "What do you want?"

The spinner is taken aback at her abruptness; she doesn't recognize him, that much is clear. She used to like him. He reminds himself of that. He manages a shy smile. "Is my brother at home?"

The woman puts her hands on her wide hips. "Walter's

got no brothers. Be off with you." She stands her ground. "Be off, I said."

The spinner's brother goes by Karl, not Walter. But the spinner knows an argument isn't in his best interests. Women alone can be talked to—but women with children, never. Plus he's lost his voice. His throat is thick; his eyes are heavy. He turns and walks down the road. Once out of sight of his brother's house, he cuts across a field and into the woods beyond, where he spends the rest of the day. With a clipped laugh, he opens the food parcel, ruefully acknowledging his own wisdom in packing it. He eats without tasting. He unties his spinning wheel and hides it under a bush. Then he rests with his back against a beech and watches the house.

At sunset a man rides up on a horse. The spinner cannot see his features well from this distance, but the man's hair is darker than Karl's. He leads the horse into a small paddock. The older child runs from the house to greet him. Then the woman comes out. The man towers over her. Karl is short, standing the height the spinner used to before he was twisted. Karl is barely a head taller than his wife. So this dark, tall man is Walter.

The spinner groans in disappointment. He sleeps in the woods.

The next day he watches the house. People come and go. But not Karl. There is no sign whatsoever of his brother.

Ten and a half years can change much.

The cold of the second night enters the spinner's bones; his rumpled leg aches. He rubs it through his pant leg and chants little songs of nonsense words:

nee and nigh and woe and why
and help the hurt that flies on by
and oh and my and oh and skry
the stilt that breaks
the world that cries

He rocks in rhythm to ease the pain. The chimney smoke from his brother's old house curls against the gray moonlit sky.

His parents died when he was still a youth. His brother is his only family—and it's anyone's guess where Karl is now. He wasn't strong. Maybe he died. After all, he coughed his way through every winter.

It's possible no one in this town remembers his name. And even if they did, what would it matter? The spinner is alone in the world, but for a daughter he's never seen—if she lived. He is cold and sad and alone. A terrific sense of exhaustion overtakes him. And with it comes the realization that he doesn't care if he's alone. After all, he's lived many years now as though he were alone, anyway.

The spinner sleeps fitfully.

In the morning he goes out to the road and walks toward town. He has eaten every bit of his food supply. All he has in the world is the spinning wheel on his back and a single skein of the finest yarn that he saved from his job at the smith's. He worked on this yarn at night, when the smith's family snored and gurgled, so that he would have a sample of his best work to show his brother. Now he'll show it to strangers, instead. A sour taste coats his tongue.

As dawn turns to morning, wagons rumble by on the

road. The spinner hopes upon hope for a ride into market. But no one returns his brief wave. He goes slowly, so slowly. His walking sticks cut into his hands. He sweats profusely by the time he reaches the market, in spite of the chill in the air.

The spinner walks the perimeter of the market. He doesn't dare try to maneuver the aisles with the spinning wheel on his back. He's liable to knock over a carefully arranged pile of fruits or cheeses. He's been whipped for less.

At last he spies a table with yarns. He unties his spinning wheel and sets it at the end of the aisle. He sits beside it with the single skein of yarn in his lap. This way if anyone is heading for the table of yarns down the aisle, they will pass him first. They will stop at his spinning wheel and see his superior work.

He loops his arm through the wheel and closes his eyes. Hunger makes him sleepy. He snoozes.

"Did you spin this yarn yourself?"

The spinner opens his eyes. The woman before him is mature, maybe thirty years old. Two boys follow her. Her eyes have no bags under them; she doesn't have the look of a weary mother. He checks her hands, which hold his yarn; sure enough, no ring. She wears a simple frock. Still, it has no worn spots, and the apron is a bit fancy, and she holds herself straight, almost haughty with importance. He is sure those boys answer to her.

The woman waits for him to speak. He can tell she's impatient from the way she holds her head, the way she turns the skein of yarn over and over.

"I did."

"What's the matter with you?"

That question leaves the spinner speechless.

"Stand up."

The spinner stands.

The woman eyes his rumpled leg. "You must be slow at spinning."

He doesn't tell her he spins with his good leg. He doesn't owe her an explanation. "I spin faster than any two other spinners put together."

"Hmmm." She pulls on the yarn, testing its strength. "Prove it. Spin."

The spinner opens his hands to both sides. "I have no fleece here."

The woman gives a curt nod. "I'll return within the hour. Stay put."

The spinner nods back. He's used to taking orders from perfect strangers. "Buy me a meal if you want me to wait."

The woman looks almost offended, but he can tell by the gleam in her eye that she's surprised more than anything. Maybe she thought he'd act grateful, the way most cripples learn to act. Maybe she likes his audacity.

He gathers his courage and points. "I want those sweet rolls over there and a sack of fruits."

The boys look at the woman with a touch of apprehension on their faces. "He doesn't know who you are," mumbles the slightly taller one.

The woman waves him into silence. She looks at the spinner steadily. "That's a high price just to make you wait. Where else might you go in the meantime? Given that you were just sleeping here a moment ago, it seems to me you'll be here whether I buy you food or not."

The spinner smiles and reaches for his yarn. He plucks it from the woman's hands with bravura and drops it back in his lap.

The woman regards him a moment longer. She withdraws a coin from her pouch, turns her back, and talks quietly to one of the boys. He runs off and returns a moment later with a small sack. The woman takes it from the boy and hands it to the spinner. "If you spin as fast as you say and if the yarn is as fine as your sample, I'll buy you a sweet roll on top of your pay." She looks down at him imperiously, then leaves.

The spinner takes out a fig, luscious southern fruit. As the gnaw in his stomach eases, he looks around the market with interest. He believes he knows the noisy fishmonger. Maybe. And the woman polishing apples. They are both close to his age.

A young blonde girl works at the table covered with yarns. She smiles enticingly at the women fingering the yarns. The spinner understands: Her job is to lure potential buyers. Maybe if he had a girl like that working for him, he could support himself through selling in the market. The customers buy the yarn, and the girl chatters to them happily; he can hear the high pitch of her voice above the calls and bargaining all around. He looks at the woman working behind the yarn table—stocky and square-jawed. The girl doesn't look much like her mother.

His eyes pass on to the old man stacking and restacking his cabbage. He might have been a neighbor. Maybe.

The spinner's a stranger here, just as he is everywhere else. He recognizes the sights and smells and sounds—but only because every marketplace in every town is the same in fundamental ways.

He's chewing the last fig when the imperious woman returns with three boys now, all three carrying heavy sacks over their shoulders. They plop them on the ground in front of the spinner.

"Spin," says the woman. "I'll do my marketing and check back with you before I leave." She points at the largest boy. "Stay here." She doesn't need to say that his job is to ensure that the spinner doesn't make off with the wool. Everyone understands that. The other two boys follow her down the aisle.

The spinner drags a sack of wool to the cattle watering trough at one corner of the market, ignoring the boy who tags at his heels and the curious eyes of strangers. He carries his spinning wheel over, as well. Then he looks around for the right rock; there are always rocks at the edge of the market for securing wagon wheels. He spies a flattish one, hobbles over, and with enormous difficulty, he pushes it to the watering trough. The boy finally makes himself useful; he picks the rock up and sets it on the edge where the spinner says. The spinner sits on the edge of the trough, as well, uses the rock to anchor his unruly leg, and spins. This way that leg cannot fly about. He will invite as little attention as he can.

Perhaps he will skip carding and simply tease the wool by hand into a thick plug, a roving, and spin it from there. That would be faster. But it's more difficult to control for uniformity in size and texture of the yarn that way.

He hand-cards the wool until he can roll it into a smooth, compact rolag to draw and twist. The long, continuous filament will make yarn the perfect thickness for a spring jacket. The spinner is no fool—he will give this woman the kind of yarn she can most use right now. Whir and spin and whir. The morning passes. He finishes the first sack of wool and works on the second.

The woman stops by to check. She smiles in delight. She dismisses the boy, who disappears down an aisle. She buys a sweet roll and hands it to the spinner without a word. He eats it, licks his fingers clean, and spins. His methodical, relentless good leg pumps the afternoon away. His other leg pulses under the rock that holds it down. He finishes the second sack, then the third. He leans back and stretches.

The woman appears from behind him. She must have been watching. She shakes her head in near disbelief. "Come. We're going to the castle." She waits a moment for the significance of her words to sink in.

The spinner isn't surprised. He had figured she worked for a noble. Indeed, she works for the highest noble.

"You will wait on the steps, and I'll bring you a bowl of whatever the servants are eating tonight."

The spinner crosses his good leg over the other, pinning it in place, and shakes his head. "Pay me. And make it a price worthy of a king's spinner."

The woman wrinkles her brow. She opens her pouch of coins. Then, on second thought, she pulls the drawstrings closed and hands the whole pouch to him. "I can give you work on a regular basis."

"I expect to leave town in the morning."

The woman rubs one shoulder as though it hurts. She speaks nonchalantly. "Just where will you go?"

The spinner knows her shoulder doesn't really hurt. He

saw her carry the sack of wool without a wince. There is nothing nonchalant in her question, despite her tone.

She leans over him, so that her face is but a hand's width from his. "You don't have anywhere to go. You don't even have a place to sleep."

He looks at her. She cannot read his mind, his eyes. She guesses. But it cuts him that she guesses right. She knows no one like him can be folded into a family or a corps of servants. The spinner refuses to blink.

The woman's eyes close just the slightest bit, giving her face a tender look. "I know a place where you can stay. It's away from everyone. In the woods."

A prickle of fear crawls up the spinner's skin. Is this what he really wants, to live away from everyone? Is he ready to give up on people entirely?

The woman lowers her voice to a whisper. "I'll bring you wool and cotton. You'll spin for me. And I'll bring you whatever supplies you ask for."

The spinner can hardly hear her for the blood throbbing in his temples. This is it. This is the end of trying. He ties the spinning wheel to his back without thinking. He takes his walking sticks and looks at the woman.

"Call me Elke," she says.

She doesn't ask his name. No one asks his name.

The spinner follows Elke away.

Nine

"WE did very well," says Saskia with enthusiasm. "We sold all the yarn. Every last skein."

"You're quite the pretty thing—everyone opens their coin pouch when you're around." Dagmar's mother looks at her. "I'll pay you a little more for today. Six extra eggs. You earned them."

Saskia shakes her head. "I don't want eggs."

Dagmar's mother gives a short laugh. "So you're asking for more money already? Cheeky thing. Are you anxious to leave me?"

Saskia catches her breath for an instant against the slap of the insult and the clutch of fear it brings. Dagmar has accused her of being uppity, and now it seems her mother shares that assessment. Though her cheeks ache from smiling all day, she smiles once more. Dagmar's family has been her lifeline. Saskia doesn't know how she'd take care of Father and herself without the small jobs they give her. Her garden yields less each day. The first frost will be upon them soon, and then there will be no food other than what Saskia can make with the milk from their two cows.

"I'm not asking for more money." Saskia clears her throat. "Would . . . would you teach me to spin?"

"Ah." Dagmar's mother looks at her sideways, and a pang of sympathy darkens her eyes. "Your mother was a spinster."

"I know. We still have her spinning wheel in the corner of Father's room."

"Well, that's a blessing." Dagmar's mother hoists her satchel higher on her shoulder and shifts her weight from foot to foot as she looks down the road. "What could be keeping them?"

Saskia touches the sleeve of Dagmar's mother's jacket. "Will you teach me, please?"

"You don't have sheep, Saskia. How will you get the wool to spin?"

"If you teach me, I can help you spin your wool. I'll learn by watching you, so you won't have to slow down at all. And I'll work at night on my mother's spinning wheel. We can sell that much more at the market. I'll take only my fair share of the money. Only . . ." What? What would be her fair share? "Only half of the price of each skein that I spin."

"Half?" Her tone scolds.

Saskia waits. She's been listening to people bargain in the market for the past half year. She knows the one making an offer is at a disadvantage.

Dagmar's mother points. "There they are." She turns to Saskia. "One-third." Then she touches her fingertips briefly to Saskia's cheek. "And if we sell out by the end of the day, an extra bit of food."

Dagmar's mother decides to teach not just Saskia, but Dagmar, too. The girls take turns at the high wheel. Saskia loves spinning, but Dagmar does not. Saskia knows why: Dagmar is clumsy-fingered; no matter how hard she concentrates, she cannot go fast, and half the fun is in going fast. Saskia, however, is nimble-fingered. One hand holds the wool, while the other deftly and continually picks little impurities from the whitish fuzz, tugs at tiny knots, teases away clumps of thickness. Within a few weeks Saskia spins as quickly and effortlessly as Dagmar's mother. She fills spindle after spindle.

In the evenings, Saskia spins at home on her mother's low wheel. It's less tiring; instead of standing and walking forward and backward in line with the spindle, as she must do with the wheel at Dagmar's house, she can sit on a stool. She rocks and hums as she spins. At first, squat candles gave her a small circle of light to work in. But once she was skilled enough, she eliminated that expense. In the dark her fingers grew intimate with the wool.

Between the two pegs that hold up the spindle runs a groove where someone must have hung the waterpot for dipping her fingers while spinning flax. The threading hook that hangs on a ribbon from the maiden has a smooth, shallow indentation in the wood near the bottom. Someone must have held it when her left hand wasn't spinning the wheel—she must have rubbed that indentation with her thumb. Reverently, Saskia holds the threading hook and presses her own thumb there as she spins, releasing it only to turn the wheel.

Whenever Father staggers by in a drunken stupor, he seems not to notice Saskia at all. If he realizes she took the spinning wheel from his room, he's never let her know. He barely talks to her.

But that's all right. Saskia has her spinning wheel.

Snow falls for the first time this season. Saskia stands in front of her house with her face turned upward and her mouth open.

"I knew you'd be outside." Dagmar appears beside her, snowflakes glistening in her hair. "Mother bet that you'd be working. But I knew even you would come outside for this snow."

Saskia laughs. "It's so big, Dagmar."

"What is?"

"The sky with no stars." Saskia spreads her arms and twirls. "Everything."

Dagmar puts a hand on her hip. "Shall we?"

Saskia hooks her arm in the crook of Dagmar's and they take their snow walk, around the mill, around the barn, through the evergreen grove, back around the defunct wheat field, which is now the sleeping vegetable garden. At the end of the hour, they arrive back at Saskia's front door.

"I need to go inside and spin."

Dagmar shakes her head with a rueful smile. She takes Saskia's hand gently. "Poor Saski. You have to work hard."

"Before, when I had to dig in the garden at dusk and dawn and then stand all day selling yarn for your mother—then, I hated it." Saskia fights the rise of pressure in her chest. "I was so angry." She stops a moment, waits until her cheeks feel cool again. "But everything changed when I learned how to spin."

"Where's your father?"

Saskia notices that Dagmar no longer calls him the miller. And why should she? He hasn't milled in so long. "In bed." She grabs Dagmar by the hand and pulls her inside. "Come watch a moment. I'll show you how my low wheel works."

Dagmar stops by the vat and wrinkles her nose at the smell of the lye. "You're soaking fleece so late at night?"

"I leave it all night. That way even the parts with dung come clean, and I can use every bit of it."

"Do you have to do everything twice as hard, twice as good as everyone else?"

Saskia thinks about how she uses only cold rainwater—never heated water, never well water—for washing, so that the wool will be softer and keep all its lanolin. She thinks about how she picks out the burrs for hours and teases the fleece gently and cards it extra fine, all of this going well beyond what Dagmar's mother taught her. "Maybe if my yarn weren't so good, we would starve."

Dagmar comes over and stands close.

Saskia takes a handful of wool from a sack. She spins, rocking far forward and far backward. "See? You do it now." She stands up.

Dagmar sits and spins. "How lovely to be off your feet." She laughs. "Your wool does spin faster." Her voice is full of genuine admiration.

Saskia nods, but she keeps thinking about that question—about why she does all this. It isn't purely the need to sell her yarns that drives her. When she spins, the wool is already so clean and smooth that she can hold it with one hand and her second hand is free to massage it as it twirls off the tip of the spindle. This way the lanolin comes forth in all its luster and softens the yarn exquisitely.

Saskia may have no mother and a drunk for a father, but she has her yarn, the best yarn she's ever seen. And that's the truth. She's not fooling herself. She has walked around the market and looked carefully at all the spinners' tables. Saskia has the power to make beauty. Spinning gives her that power.

Saskia takes Dagmar's hair and flicks away the melting snow. She braids Dagmar's locks lovingly. A scarf should grace this hair. A scarf of the softest yarn ever. Saskia is poor, but she has the means to give a wonderful Christmas gift. Yes.

Ten

DAGMAR stamps her feet to warm them. "The winds are strong today." She pulls her scarf, the one Saskia knitted her, tighter around her ears.

"But they sell our yarns." Saskia blinks against the cold.

An old woman wraps a strand of Saskia's yarn round and round her hand, until it covers it entirely. She holds it to her cheek. "Soft like a mother's breast," she says.

This woman's mother must have died many years ago. And her own breasts probably hang empty against her ribs. There is something terribly sad in her words. Saskia suddenly puts the skein in her arms. "One-third off, for you."

The woman buys it and leaves.

"You're crazy." Dagmar pinches Saskia. "One-third off— that means you earned nothing from that skein."

"It doesn't matter. It was my last one."

Dagmar rearranges a couple of skeins on her pile. "You don't have to rub it in."

"That's not what I meant and you know it." Saskia hugs herself inside her cloak. "I'll go shopping now. Meet you back here in time to go home together?"

She goes first to the butcher and buys a beef bone with enough meat attached to flavor a stew. Then she bargains for yesterday's leftover cabbage. She does well. Tonight she and Father will have a hot, filling meal, and she still has three coins in her pocket.

Saskia saves coins. By mid-January, she has the money to buy her own wool. She visits sheep farms and chooses the wool most pungent with lanolin to spin thick yarn for sweaters and blankets. She chooses creamy sheep and the occasional and prized black sheep to spin fine wool for shirts and trousers and frocks. Others dye their wools with roots and berries, but Saskia prefers the natural colors. In fact, she loves the naturalness of the wool so much that every now and then she spins skeins that are full of slubs, for knitting sweaters that will come bumpy and stout like the sheep themselves. Her earnings from these special yarns is higher than from the wool she spins for Dagmar's family.

Saskia and Father make it from day to day this way: She's a slave; he's a ghost. Her mouth is bilious with contained reproach.

It is February. Saskia wakes before dawn and spins. Father snores. Saskia gets up from the spinning wheel and goes into Father's room. Her palm itches, and she knows she wants to yank the covers off him and slap his face.

She goes outside to the cellar where the jugs of gin are stacked. Since learning to spin, she hasn't been his lackey for gin, so she doesn't know what remains of his supply. She's appalled now: There are still so many. At this rate, Father can drink away another year perhaps.

Saskia grabs a jug and throws it on the ground. The cork comes loose. Gin flows free. Her temples pound. A waste. But, oh, it's right. She stashes the jug in the bottom of her rucksack. She will sell a jug—an empty jug—at market today and every day. Her tongue is so thick with danger that she can hardly close her mouth.

Saskia leans out the window and smells the snow. The smell changes as winter wanes. She thinks about the hoe that sleeps under the lean-to on the side of the house. Soon she will dig. She'll still tend the herb garden. But her main job will be the large vegetable garden. She will plant lettuces first, then peas, then in the hot weather, green squash.

The day warms a little. Saskia goes outside, draws a bucket from the well, and drinks long of the freezing water. That's when she sees Father. He's on his face in the snow outside the cellar door.

Saskia rolls him onto his back. His breath still comes, but his skin is as cold as the snow. She works her arm under his back and tries to lug him toward the house, but his dead weight is too much for her. In the end, she drags him.

She sets the fire to roaring and rubs his face, arms, legs, chest, till the color returns.

For a good week, Father drifts in and out of a restless sleep. He coughs most of the time. He cannot hold down food. Eventually, Saskia feeds him nothing but broth. He moans. She rubs him warm when he shivers; she rubs him with snow when the fever returns.

Then one morning she wakes, realizing she's gone

through the whole night without being woken by a rack of coughs. The feeling of being truly rested elates her. Saskia goes outside and stands with her face turned upward, caressed by the blessed sunlight. After a while, she draws a bucket of water from the well and goes inside to make broth.

Father stands in the common room, looking confused. "Who spins, daughter?" His voice is clear, if weak.

"I do, Father."

He looks at her in wonder. "How did you learn to spin?"

Her cheeks heat with the surprise of his attention. She's wary.

He picks up a skein of rare black yarn. "Did you do this?"

"Yes." Right before your eyes, she thinks.

He feels the yarn thoughtfully. "You could sell it."

"I do already, Father. I've done it since late last spring."

He walks to the window and makes a smacking noise with his lips. "You've fed us both with the profits from your spinning since then?"

"Not just from spinning." She thinks of the jugs she sells every day now. But what point is there in provoking him? "I sold squash in summer and early fall."

"You've been resourceful, daughter." Father goes to the small sack of salt beside the hearth. He puts in a finger, then rubs his teeth with the coarse white-gray crystals. He runs his hands through his hair, combing in a crude way. He looks around for a cloth to clean himself with; Saskia already holds a wet one out to him. He takes it and presses it to his neck, under his beard.

Father walks outside in nothing but his shirt and

trousers. Saskia watches from the window. He goes to his cellar, opens the door, stands looking for a while. How much can he know? She is sure this is the first time he's been sober in months. He comes back inside, empty-handed. "Five jugs remain," he announces. "Only five jugs from my whole stockpile." He takes a deep breath. "It's a wonder I'm not dead."

"You almost did die, Father. You've been ill for the past week. It was awful."

"I'm what's awful." Father's voice halts with shame. "But I'm lucky; I have a second chance. And, thank the Lord, I still have you."

Saskia holds on to the middle shell of the necklace she wears. She rubs it gently between thumb and forefinger, her breath curled carefully in her mouth. Her skin tingles with hope.

"I'll take these skeins to market, daughter. You stay here and spin. I'll bring back whatever other plants I can find—maybe someone will be selling flax and cotton from the south already this year. This wheel is suitable for any fiber." He takes off his shirt as he talks and reaches for the clean one.

Saskia breathes deep at last. She cannot relax. Not yet. She must stay strong, just in case. Father's change of heart may be sincere—for, yes, he did almost die. But she cannot know how long it will last.

Still, she feels something hard inside her start to yield.

PART THREE

Yarn

Eleven

ELKE comes brusquely through the woods. The spinner recognizes her sounds. After all, no one else comes this way except the occasional hunter—and hunters move with stealth. Elke comes boldly and always alone. She doesn't even bring the boys who helped her in the market the day he met her. She seems to have the idea that the spinner prefers solitude, though she has never asked him directly.

He pulls the bench out through the door of his shack. It is his only furniture other than his spinning wheel. He sits in the sun that saturates the little clearing where he cooks his dinners. He waits for her.

Each time she comes, she picks up the yarn he's already spun and leaves him a sack of fibers—wool or flax or cotton—to be spun for the next time. He easily spins the amount of yarn she requires between each visit. Elke brings the stuff of his desolation.

And each time she comes, she brings news of bake fairs and a traveling circus troupe, of threats from nearby kingdoms and new alliances that void them. Elke brings the world beyond these woods, as well.

The curious part is that, even though he lives near the town he grew up in, he has no interest in the particular people there. It is more human company in general that he aches for. But only now and then. And less frequently all the time. These days it takes special news from Elke to awaken that interest.

Elke appears at last, picking pine needles from her hair. "Hello, my little man."

Is the spinner her little man? Sometimes he is almost sure that she wishes he was. The way she touches her hair now, the turn of her wrist, the vulnerable angle of her elbow as she tries to make herself more presentable—these details seem to betray an affection. In the four years that he has known her, she has changed her manner toward him, from the efficient headmistress of the castle to a woman who can be tentative. And she has aged noticeably. Her cheeks are drawn; the corners of her eyes and the curves of her upper lip radiate small lines in her pale, dry skin.

Yet it is not her dryness that weighs down the spinner's hands so that his never brush hers. It is the memory of the slow luxury of afternoon love in the barn loft with the young woman fifteen years ago. The remembered sensation of being a bead of sap on a balsam fir that heats in the sun and finally bursts, only to gradually drip away. These memories leave him with a loss that throbs long into the night.

And it is the nagging fear that maybe he is wrong about

Elke. His hermetic lifestyle exacts a price: He's losing the ability to gauge people from their comportment. So maybe the blue lines on Elke's wrist are turned toward him not to invite a kiss, but just because that's the way she moves. Maybe the softness that comes into her eyes now and then is nothing more than pity. The spinner got tired of pity so long ago it seems like another lifetime.

Elke sets a large sack on the ground beside his bench and places a small sack on the edge of the bench. He knows the small sack contains food. "Should I leave the wool sack here, or do you want me to carry it inside?"

It's true that the spinner weakens. But he can still lug a sack of fibers into the shack. Plus he doesn't like the idea of Elke entering his home and seeing how bare he keeps it, how spartan his life is. "Here."

Elke sits beside him on the bench. "Curt today, are you? Well, I've got something that should get your cold blood flowing." She smiles just the slightest bit, but her face lights up, the balls of her cheeks tighten. The spinner's breath quickens. She unpins a fold in her skirt and takes out a skein of wool.

Disappointment splatters like mud on a new cloak. The spinner is about to ask how wool yarn could possibly interest him, when the sun catches the strand that Elke holds out to him. It sparkles off the white and goes thick and warm on the black. The spinner takes the skein with respectful hands. "Black and white together," he says, admiration making his voice rich.

"I knew you'd be impressed." Elke interweaves her fingers. "I knew it." Her eyes sparkle happily.

The spinner is full of questions. Yet he bites his tongue. This master spinner presents danger. The spinner's present arrangement with Elke depends on her preferring his yarn over all others'. He places the skein on the bench by Elke.

"Ask me." Elke rocks a little on her skinny buttocks in repressed excitement. Her white underskirt below her gray frock always shows a little, but now she seems to notice it for the first time. She reaches down and pulls the hem of her frock lower. Then she clasps her hands around one knee in a mixture of primness and almost flirtatiousness. She turns to him and lets out her full smile. "You're bursting with questions."

"Then answer them."

"This spinner hawks it for making children's sweaters. The black and white twist around each other irregularly, so that the sweaters come out mottled. They look lively, and everyone is buying this yarn. We have no children in the castle, of course. But I bought some just for fun." She lets go of her knee and sits upright. "And to show you, of course."

The spinner nods to himself. This yarn is absolutely right for children's sweaters. The unknown spinner has a mind for business as well as mastery of the skill.

Elke leans toward him as though she reads his mind. But then, anyone could read his mind right now. "It's a simple girl," crows Elke. "Fourteen years old."

"New to town?"

"No. She's been spinning for years, but then I haven't bothered to look at the yarns in the market since you came. She spins wool and flax and cotton, just like you do." Elke's voice is warm, loving. She doesn't seem to realize that the spinner isn't pleased at hearing this. "But she also spins rabbit hair and fox hair and any kind of animal hair."

"What's her name?"

"I didn't ask."

The spinner jumps from the bench and stands before Elke. "You asked her all these things and you didn't even show the courtesy to ask her name?"

"I didn't speak with her." Elke draws back defensively. She picks at the scalloped edge of her apron. "I spoke with her father." Her eyes search his. "Why does it matter so much? A name is just a name."

A name is a person, the spinner wants to say. A name is an emblem of worthiness. He sinks back onto the bench in a turmoil of fascination and fear. When he trusts his voice not to break, he says, "Tell me about the father."

"His name is Christof," Elke answers swiftly.

The spinner laughs in spite of himself. "All right, so you asked his name. Tell me about him."

"He boasts his daughter's praises in the most distasteful way—he's loud and exaggerated. And he stinks." Elke wrinkles her nose at the memory. "He was sober when I talked with him in the market. But I could smell the drink on his clothes."

"Many men drink every night." The spinner thinks back over all the families he lived with during the ten years he was an itinerant spinner. "Maybe most men."

"I suspect he drinks more than most. It wears on him. He looks old enough to be the girl's grandfather."

"Maybe he is."

"He called the spinster his daughter. And from his grooming, I am quite sure he's a widower."

"So he comes to market every day and sells yarn, while the daughter stays at home and spins?"

"He comes but twice a week. On the other days, he runs his mill."

The spinner's throat seems to cave in. For a second he cannot breathe. Christof the miller. Christof would be an old man by now. He was old even fifteen years ago, when the young woman married him.

The spinner stares at the wool on the bench beside him. The world grows dim. Tiny lights dance before his eyes, as though the yarn transforms itself into a starry sky. The miller has a daughter. The miller's daughter spun this yarn, this starry yarn.

The girl lives.

His girl.

The spinner falls forward into the stars.

"What's the matter?" Elke holds him to her now, her thin arms circling his narrow shoulders. "Are you ill?"

Her chest gives off the sweetness of mint and a hint of camphor. The spinner breathes deeply.

He straightens and pulls himself free of her.

Elke smoothes the cloth of her bodice, though it shows no signs of having been disturbed. "Are you all right now?" She looks away.

The spinner hasn't been all right for years.

Elke looks at him again and gives a small smile. "At least the color is returning to your face." Her laugh is quick and tentative. "I expected you to like her wool, but I didn't expect you to swoon over it."

The spinner picks up the skein with both hands. He tucks it inside his shirt, near his heart.

"Ah, so you're playing the thief now? What a pity. I'd just decided to make you a gift of it, and there you go and steal it before I've even had the chance to offer it properly."

The spinner hugs himself, as though protecting the yarn from Elke. Had she really intended it as a gift? Can she begin to guess what it means to him?

She stands now. "That yarn is fine quality but still not as fine as what you spin." She smiles softly. "In the sack you'll find black wool and white wool. You can spin playful yarns, too. And yours will be better."

So Elke has sensed his conflict, after all. The spinner shakes his head. He doesn't want to compete with the young spinster.

Elke reaches out a hand as though to touch the spinner on the shoulder, then lets it hover in the air. "Are you worried? You have such a fine spinning wheel. You'll always do better work than the miller's daughter. I'm sure her spinning wheel is nothing compared to yours."

The spinner's head spins as fast as his spinning wheel. Elke in her misguided attempt to encourage and console him has made everything more complicated. He tries to imagine the spinster—a smaller version of her mother, perhaps—sitting down on a stool, drawing it up close to the spinning wheel. The wheel that the young woman used to work at. Oh, that spinning wheel. "Does she spin on her mother's wheel?"

"What?" Elke's mouth stays open for a second. "How would I know?"

"Ask."

Elke holds her elbows in her hands with a look of consternation. "Why?"

"Ask. And find out if her mother's dead."

"What are you talking about?"

The spinner wasn't even sure himself, but now the idea comes clear to him. "Take my spinning wheel to her, and if she spins on her dead mother's wheel, then exchange mine for hers."

"What? You don't know anything about this girl."

"I think I do."

Elke shakes her head in confusion. "You want to give up your perfect wheel for hers? Hers could be rickety and wobbly and who knows what."

I will feel my beloved's hands every time I touch the wood, he thinks. "Take mine. Bring me back her mother's. This very evening."

"But what will I say? How will I explain to this girl that a twisted little man wants to exchange wheels with her?"

The spinner's ears ring as though they've been boxed. Her affection is nothing more than pity, after all. "Don't describe me. Say an admirer offers an exchange. That's all. An admirer."

"She'll be alarmed. What young woman wouldn't be frightened at some unknown admirer who extends such an offer?"

"Then make something up," barks the spinner. "Take the wheel. Go."

"I can't carry the wheel and all the yarn you've spun as well."

"Leave the yarn. When you bring me back the girl's wheel, you can take it."

Elke nods. "It's all so strange."

"Do it."

She lowers her shoulders in resignation. "All right."

The spinner hobbles into the shack and comes out holding the spinning wheel.

Elke takes it awkwardly with both hands.

"I'll tie it to your back," says the spinner.

"I'll carry it this way."

The spinner nods.

Elke walks away.

"And ask her name," calls the spinner. "Ask her name."

Elke is gone now, out of hearing range.

He reaches into his shirt and pulls out the skein. He tosses it lightly with both hands, chanting, chanting:

> wool and flax and cotton
> spin the fingers bare
> hare and fox
> skin and bones
> in me on me in me on me
> oh what spin what yarn what harm

He digs his fingers deep into the yarn, the precious yarn his daughter has spun.

Twelve

IT'S a good trade." Father's voice is gruff.

Saskia has to be careful. She's fought with Father only a handful of times over the past few years, but each time it has precipitated a drinking binge with a bout in bed. If she can just manage to get through this without an open confrontation, maybe Father can keep to his routine of working by day and drinking only by night. With the exception of the ten months that he stayed in bed constantly and the few months after that, when he stayed sober constantly, that alternation of working days and drinking nights has been Father's routine all Saskia's life. The only thing that ever upsets the routine is a fight with Saskia.

She stands in front of her spinning wheel. "I like the wheel I have, Father." She speaks with gentle firmness, not at all how she feels. The sound of her own voice irritates her; she is tired of the maneuvering she is about to do even before it begins.

"It wobbles."

"Not much. And I can cure it with a simple piece of leather if it bothers you. The wheel is straight, Father. Not a hint of warp." Saskia hesitates, then decides to use everything in her power. "It was Mother's spinning wheel, and I love it."

Father's eyes go blank. Then he sighs. "Don't be stubborn. The woman who asked for the exchange works for the king. The king, Saskia. She's taken an interest in you. She even wanted to know your name."

"My name? Why?"

"She likes you. Don't be such a thick skull. She says you'll make even finer yarns on this spinning wheel. And look at it, Saskia, look." Father pulls the spinning wheel from the center of the room, where he set it when he first brought it home. He places it in front of Saskia. "See?"

The blond wood looks warm, Saskia has to admit. She reaches out a tentative hand and touches the wheel lightly. It spins smooth as warm milk, more smoothly than Mother's wheel even after it's just been oiled. "I don't understand why a complete stranger wants this exchange. This wheel is worth much more than mine."

"Enough! It doesn't matter why. She's expecting me at the market. I already agreed to the trade."

"It's a poor trade for her, Father."

"So what? Maybe she's foolish. It's probably not even her money—it's the king's. He has money to spare."

Saskia doesn't speak.

"Anyway," says Father, his voice rising in irritation, "why should you care?"

It feels so strange. The exchange is tantamount to a gift. Saskia wouldn't trust any gift unless it came from someone who loved her. She has some sense of the ways of the world.

She touches the wheel again. It spins absolutely silently. Her old wheel makes little groans now and then.

Saskia fills a distaff with flax and pulls her stool up to the new wheel. Morning lights the room brightly. She spins. The linen yarn practically appears on its own. She spins and spins. When Saskia looks up, Father is gone. Her old spinning wheel is gone. She rushes to the door and stares down the empty road.

She returns to the wheel, picking pod husks from cotton. She spins a cotton skein. The wheel moves as effortlessly with cotton as with flax and as quietly. And the yarn itself appears more sinuous, more alluring. She imagines rich ladies dining at fancy tables and dancing in fancy halls, dressed in gowns made of this yarn.

It is late afternoon by now. Saskia rises and stands beside the wheel. She turns the ring on her finger. She touches the shell necklace that she rubs so often the ribs have worn smooth. Two gifts from Mother. Her hands itch to touch the indentation in the threading hook of Mother's wheel. Her ears long to hear its soft noise—not groans at all, but its own soothing music.

Saskia runs outside and drops to her knees, panting in the middle of the high grasses in the small meadow beyond the wheat field. She yanks at the autumn-dry grasses as she tries to slow her breathing, swallow her tears. She fills the scoop of her skirt with the sweet-smelling grasses. The memory of her and Dagmar shaving Father and holding his hairs in the scoop of their shifts flashes before her. She was frightened then. But she's not frightened now. She can use the new wheel to right the terrible wrong of giving up Mother's wheel.

Saskia races back to the house. She chooses white wool and spins with one hand while, with the other, she gradually feeds in thin stalks of dry meadow grass, making sure that the wool completely covers each blade of grass. She spins a full skein and rubs the yarn across her ankle. It's more substantial than plain wool. She holds it to her nose. The smell suggests lazy afternoons in late summer, when the morning's haying is done and the sun is too high to allow any more work. The smell envelops deliciously. And the natural lanolin of the wool will keep the water out when it's washed so the grasses inside the yarn won't rot. In fact, the lanolin will release more of the grass fragrance.

Yes, Saskia can make new yarns, yarns like no one has ever thought of before. She can sell them at extra-high prices. She can save her profits in the coin box she hides under the bed. And then she can go to the castle and buy back her mother's spinning wheel.

The next day Saskia picks rye stalk. At first she thinks of adding it to cotton for increased durability and flexibility. But cotton fiber is only the length of her thumb at best—rye is much longer. It will be too difficult to blend them. Instead, she spins the rye stalk in with flax. The raw linen alone would be pale honey-colored, but with rye added to it, it yields a warm brown. It will sell well.

The day after that, Saskia rolls fruit fiber in spiderweb. When she was little, she cringed at spiders, but now she admires the intricacy of their weaving. She is convinced that spider silk will help hold the fruit fiber fast, and she loves its springiness. This mix spins with flax easily. The linen comes with colored soft bumps. It is playful and dancy and makes her laugh. A few months of spinning like this, and she'll have enough money, yes, she will.

When she wakes the next morning, she picks the tiny wild violets that thrive among the meadow grasses. She removes the velvet flesh of the petals, leaving only the tiny stamen and pistils. Now she turns to the leaves. With her thumbnail, she separates the thin veins from the rest. She spins a skein of cotton, adding to it the violet stamen and pistils and veins. She plies two strands together for extra strength. The cotton cloth will come thicker, of course, but still soft.

She works all week. When she is through, the pile of skeins is high and fragrant and colorful. She and Father take them to market. People stop at her table and sniff and exclaim in delight. Every one of them buys without regret, even when Father refuses to bargain on the price.

Father leaves Saskia to tend the table herself and disappears in the crowd.

A skinny woman comes to the table. She tilts her head at Saskia and smiles. "Is this your father's stall?"

Saskia nods.

The woman's fingers absentmindedly pick at the scalloped edges of her apron. "Did you spin these yarns?"

"Yes," says Saskia.

The woman picks up a skein that has fruit fibers mixed with flax. She inspects it. Then her eyes scan the six separate piles. "I'll take one of each." She pays without hesitation. "You're better than I ever would have guessed." She leaves, her booted feet kicking through the bit of underskirt that shows from beneath her gray frock.

Saskia is puzzled by the woman's abrupt words. But the coins in her hand are heavy.

Ha! At the rate she's making money, Saskia will be able to buy back Mother's spinning wheel by Christmas. Ha!

Thirteen

T H E spinner rolls his head from side to side on his pillow of yarns. Over the last few weeks, he has entreated Elke to bring him an enormous bundle of them. He has taken some of his own yarn and tied it around the skeins of Saskia's yarn. He sleeps with the textures and aromas his daughter has created.

He loves this Saskia, this blonde girl whom Elke describes to him in such detail. He wants to go to the market and talk with her.

For the hundredth time, he imagines their first meeting. Saskia is surprised by his appearance. She looks away. He catches her glancing out of the corner of her eye. He waits, unmoving, his face calm. Slowly she turns to him and looks carefully. She is used to looking carefully—he knows that from the yarns she spins. Her intelligent eyes seek an answer. She finds it in his rumpled leg. The slant of his hips, of his shoulders, of his eyes—all of it follows from that one leg. She isn't afraid of him. And she isn't repulsed.

He talks to her about her yarns. He reveals himself as a spinner, too. They move with care, but assurance, into the realm they both master. Before long, they share secrets of the trade.

She delights in his experience, as he delights in her playful creativity.

Her eyes lengthen his leg, uncurl his chest. They plump his withered heart.

He comes and talks to her every day. And then he tells her. He tells her who he really is. She cries and opens her arms. She says she should have known, for she saw herself in him.

He hobbles into her embrace.

It is the truth of this hobbling that shakes him from this reverie.

The spinner knows that he doesn't ever really want to talk with Saskia. He doesn't ever want to see the revulsion in her eyes that would surely come at the sight of him. He doesn't want to face her disbelief and disgust if he lost control of himself and revealed his identity.

He gets up from his bedroll and stretches his rounded spine, one limb too long, one limb too short. Then he goes outside to relieve himself. He comes back in, grabs a handful of wool, and spins. The dead woman's spinning wheel feels like a friend of sorts. He caresses the wood. He leans forward and touches his lips to it.

He cries.

PART FOUR

Gold

Fourteen

SASKIA works day after day, filling the yarn orders that keep coming. She's so busy with her own yarns that she doesn't work for Dagmar's family anymore.

And she's better friends with Dagmar for it. They meet on Sunday afternoons to walk and talk. Dagmar will wed soon and go to live in the house of her in-laws. Of her three older brothers, all but Stefan are married now, so it was only natural for her father to make arrangements next for Dagmar.

The new life ahead is all Dagmar talks about. That's why their friendship has deepened. Dagmar is no longer jealous of Saskia's beauty. Nor is she jealous of the yarns Saskia spins. She is in love. They hook arms and laugh as they walk.

Saskia knows both joy for her friend and envy of the love Dagmar has. But the envy is silly. She reminds herself she hasn't the slightest interest in any of the youths she knows, even if Father did have a dowry to offer. Indeed, if Saskia wanted a husband, she could offer a dowry herself. But right now, buying back Mother's spinning wheel is more important.

Saskia goes to the window. She rests her arms there and leans out. Birds swoop around the wild rose bush. Such a smart place to put a nest, all protected by thorns. Forsythia and azalea scent the air and pleasure the eyes. Spring bursts in all its fullness. It will be her birthday soon—her fifteenth birthday. Saskia feels the shells on her necklace.

Did Mother visit the sea? Did she make this necklace?

Did a suitor perhaps give them to her on her fifteenth birthday?

A restlessness seizes Saskia, though it is not yet even full morning. She will go to Dagmar's for a surprise visit.

Saskia drapes a light shawl over her shoulders and opens the front door.

A horse-drawn wagon rumbles into view. Father returns already, and he left for market only an hour ago. He pulls the horse to a halt. "Climb up, Saskia. Hurry." He smiles through his beard, but he himself climbs down. His movements are quick and happy. He laughs.

Father's lightheartedness so surprises Saskia that it spreads to her. She climbs onto the bench seat at the front. Her foot knocks against a jug. It's a beer jug. Father has taken to brewing beer in the last year. "Where are we going, Father?"

He laughs again and runs into the house. A few moments later, he appears carrying her spinning wheel high over his head, as though he is a young man, strong and agile. He puts it in the back of the wagon.

In alarm, Saskia climbs over into the back of the wagon. "What are you doing?"

He puts his face so close to hers that she can smell his breath. He's been drinking already. "We're going to the castle."

Saskia stands beside her spinning wheel, holding on. She wants to ask why, why has he been drinking in the morning, why are they going to the castle, but Father has disappeared into the house again.

He comes out a moment later, a large sack over his shoulder. He throws it into the wagon, then climbs onto the front bench. He picks up the jug and drinks long. "Sit up here with me."

"I'm staying by my spinning wheel."

"That's a good idea," he says happily. "You hold on to it. Nothing bad must happen to it."

Saskia sits. What sort of scheme has he contrived? She opens the sack. It holds skeins of her yarn. "Why are we going to the castle?" She clutches at the legs of the spinning wheel possessively. "Is it something to do with that woman who took Mother's spinning wheel? Is it her again?"

"No."

"Then what, Father? Tell me."

"You're going to spin for the king."

"The king?"

Father clicks his tongue, and the horse starts up. "That woman who exchanged wheels bought a lot of your yarn last week. She . . ."

"I knew it was her! I don't like her."

"You've never even met her. And it isn't her, anyway. All

she did was have your yarn woven into leggings for the king, and then His Majesty himself couldn't help but notice the colors. Your yarn covers the king, Saskia."

"And the king came to talk to you?"

"Of course not. The woman sent a servant to the market for me. She wanted more yarn exactly like the yarn in the leggings. But your yarn is never the same. I told her that. I told her you keep making new and better yarns. The best yarns in the world."

Saskia isn't pleased at Father's high praise. He often embarrasses her with his exaggerations. "Am I supposed to spin yarn that matches the leggings? Is that it? And what yarn was it, Father? Did it have flowers in it? What if I can't get hold of the same flowers right now? What . . ."

"Hush, Saskia. The king himself summons you. You, my daughter. You, the master spinster."

"Oh!" Saskia holds on to the spinning wheel as they bump along the road.

Fifteen

THE king sits in an ordinary chair at a large table. He looks at Father expectantly, his young face neither haughty nor friendly. A manservant stands behind and to one side of his chair, his face blank. The king speaks: "You're a miller?"

Father nods.

"You told my servant your daughter spins the best yarn in the world." The king's voice is testy; his words, a challenge. Saskia shrinks farther behind Father.

Father nods again. Perhaps he's lost his voice. That's a good thing, at least. That way he can't boast.

"Show me, miller."

Father opens the sack of skeins. He stares within a long time. Finally, he puts one on the table.

The king unwinds it a bit, strokes it. "Fine wool."

Father fumbles around, takes out a second skein.

The king strokes. "Superior linen."

Father takes out a third skein and a fourth, this time quickly, with assurance. Saskia imagines she can see his chest puffing out.

The king smiles now. "And may I see this accomplished spinster?" His voice is half teasing as he cranes to see past Father.

Saskia fingers the shell necklace. Father nudges her with his elbow. She steps forward reluctantly and curtsies.

The king looks her up and down. His eyes linger rudely where they will.

Saskia feels as though she is a skein of yarn herself, lying on a table in the market, helpless against anyone's hands. She wants to run.

The king lowers his brow and beckons her forth with a curved finger. "Show me your hands."

Saskia approaches, holding out both hands, her arms straight and rigid, her palms facing down.

The king feels her hands all over. "Soft, as a spinster's should be."

Saskia withdraws a step and fights the urge to clasp her hands behind her back. Of course her hands are soft; they work with lanolin every day. Did he doubt she was a spinster? It is not remarkable to be a spinster.

The king walks to the sack of skeins and puts both hands in up to his elbows. He laughs. "Your yarns are unusual." He puts a skein on the table and combs his beard with his fingers. "What's this?"

Saskia goes to speak, but her voice won't come. She clears her throat and starts again. "I mixed grasses into the wool."

He pulls out another skein. "And this?"

"Parts of heartsease mixed in . . ."

"Heartsease?" He winds the yarn around his fingers. "What's that?"

"Flowers, Your Majesty. Simple wild flowers. But they're cheerful. They come in purples and yellows."

Father nods enthusiastically. "She's a wizard with fibers. She can do anything."

The king's eyes widen. "Anything?" His tone is dismissive.

"She transforms ordinary plants into amazing yarns."

Saskia squirms. She wants to pinch Father into silence.

The king's face registers annoyance. "It takes a lot to amaze a king." He unweaves the yarn from his fingers and tosses it onto the table. "Much more than flower-speckled yarns. I clothe myself in finery the likes of which you've never felt."

"My daughter's yarns clothe the ladies you dance with. Their sheen dazzles your eyes."

"Not much dazzles my eyes. I've seen spectacular sights you'll never even dream."

"My daughter's yarn is more than spectacular; it's precious."

"I'm surrounded with precious things," snaps the king. "Everywhere you look, there's gold. But a man of your station wouldn't even recognize it."

"I know gold." Father's words are rapid and loud.

"And how is that, miller?"

"My daughter can spin straw into gold."

The king's face goes red. "Do you presume to mock your king?"

Father shakes his head; his finally silent mouth hangs ajar.

"You brought the spinning wheel, as I ordered, did you not?"

Father nods.

"Then your daughter will prove your words. She can make me richer than ever."

Father looks at Saskia now, his eyes seeking.

Saskia's head spins. She would fall but for the support of Father's arm. She must have grabbed him during the volley of boasts. But she doesn't want to touch him now. She drops her hand and stares at him determinedly. It is Father who got them into this trouble. He has to find the way out.

Father looks back at the king. "Excuse me, Your Majesty, but . . ."

"I'll fill a room with straw," the king announces loudly, as though he's holding forth before a crowded court. He steps toward Saskia and looms over her. "And you, lass, will stay in that room. You have till tomorrow morning to spin all the straw into gold. A roomful of gold!"

The crazy, unreal words stun Saskia.

The king puts a finger to his lips to hush her before she has a chance to get out even a single word. "If you fail, you must die. Such is the price of trying to make a fool of your king." The king touches the tip of one of Saskia's locks. "The color of your hair entices, little spinster. I'd more believe you could turn these locks into gold." He leaves the room, his royal robe fanning out behind.

The servant remains, impassive, before the doorway.

Saskia looks at her father. He stares back at her. Her eyes fill with tears. She whispers, "How could you say that, Father?"

"I don't know." He is shaking his head, aghast. "I don't know."

"You're not drunk. Not completely." She wails quietly now. "You have no excuse." Her voice rises, reedy and thin. "How could you?"

"It came to me." Father pulls at his hair. He teeters and smacks the back of his head against the wall. "Your mother, it's your mother's fault. She's betrayed me yet again."

"My mother? Stop this idiotic talk." Saskia twists her hands. "Oh, Father, look what you've done. You've condemned me."

"She told me." Father's voice pleads for understanding. His hands are lost in his hair now, and he's turning circles like a madman. "She spoke of someone she knew who once spun straw into gold." His voice screeches. "She said . . ." He stops and shakes his head. "Oh, daughter."

Saskia feels woozy. Sick. She will die in the morning.

Father blinks many times. Then he grabs Saskia by the upper arms. He squeezes so hard she would scream if pain mattered now. "You must try, Saskia. If someone else could do it, so can you."

"No one can do it, Father," Saskia whispers in horror. "Straw is not gold."

Sixteen

SASKIA walks around the room of straw. It is a small room, the size of the room she sleeps in at home. The size alone would be a comfort, were it not for all this waiting straw that taunts her. She searches through the bales. Something, anything, might hold an answer.

There is one high window in this room. She stacks two bales of straw, climbs up, and looks out. The room of straw is mostly underground. The bars over this window are set a hand's width apart. She presses her head against them so hard her temples want to crack.

She walks around the room again. She stops at the door, knocks. She pulls on it yet again. The window, the door, the walls, the floor—she has felt everywhere for a means of escape.

She stands by the door and pleads once more, "Please. Please may I speak with the king?"

She remembers how the king looked at her. He seemed interested, greedy, lustful perhaps, but not cruel. Why is he doing this? It was a stupid competition—a silly thing that got out of hand. He can't believe Father's rash boast. No one can spin straw into gold. Father was foolish, not malicious. "Please," she shouts. She bangs both fists on the door. "I must speak with the king."

She leans her back against the door. Panic makes her pant.

She tries to slow her violent heart. She needs to think. Saskia has been in trouble before. And Father has been the source of that trouble. Her head has carried her through. Her head and hard work. She must be calm.

Father said Mother told him of someone who spun straw into gold. Was Mother mad?

Is there something Saskia doesn't understand about straw? Straw is long and strong. And the color isn't that far from gold. With enough kneading, perhaps . . . But what is she thinking? Straw is straw.

Yet how else can she think? And fibers change so much in the spinning. Flax becomes linen, after all. Still, gold?

Saskia sits at the spinning wheel. She takes a handful of straw and pumps the pedal.

Bits of driest straw break away. They sting her eyes. She grabs another handful of straw and bends the stalks around her fingers, trying to make them flexible. She spins fast. She spins slow. She prays. She thinks of nothing. The straw splinters and pricks her hands. She grabs more straw and spins, this time not just bending the straw, but spitting on it as well—anything to help the straw bend. She pulls strands of hair from her head and twines them around the straw stalks, for didn't the king himself suggest that? She spins. Straw dust coats her. Sudden sneezes throw her onto the floor.

The room goes dark. Saskia rushes to the window. Evening does not yet fall; it is only a cloud covering the sun. Saskia has the rest of the afternoon. Then the evening. Then the night.

For what?

In the morning, she will die.

She runs the fingers of one hand lightly over the other. They are chapped from the dry straw, dry as her eyes. Her left index finger is grooved on the side between the second and third joints, where the yarn pulls as she spins. Working hands. Productive hands. All for naught.

Why, why must she die?

And now her eyes are no longer dry.

Saskia lies on the floor with walls of straw on three sides and the spinning wheel at her feet. Her fifteenth birthday will come but a week and two days from now. She twists the ring on her finger round and round and prays to the spirit of her mother. She rocks herself. Her teeth chatter. Her bones ache.

Seventeen

THEY lie in a line across the clean blanket spread out on the floor: the treadle, the footman, the wheel, the driving band, the pulleys, the bobbin. The spinner rubs each part with sheep tallow and polishes them with a soft cloth. Then he reassembles the spinning wheel. As he tightens the tension screw, Elke appears in the open doorway.

She isn't supposed to be here now. If he had known she was coming, he'd have been outside waiting for her. He coughs to give himself a moment to prepare the rough speech she deserves, when he takes in her stricken face. All anger disappears. "What is it? What has happened?"

"Something that will grieve you." Elke leans against the open door frame as if for support. Her knees buckle, and she falls.

The spinner hobbles to her side and drapes one of her arms around his shoulders. "Come sit on the bench."

Elke stumbles across the room with him and sits heavily on the bench. "Oh, my poor little man." She looks down and talks as if to her hands. "I didn't mean it to happen."

The spinner stands in front of her and waits. There is little in the outside world that concerns him, yet a blanket of doom descends now. "Speak."

"I had no idea it would come to this. I know you're going to be upset. I know . . ." Her voice trails off.

So Elke betrayed him somehow. Does this mean he'll have to go back to the life of a wanderer? He waits.

"I wanted different cloth. Not that your yarn isn't wonderful. Yours is wonderful. It is. But I don't know, I just wanted something new. I didn't intend anything wrong. I . . ."

"Don't speak around it, Elke."

Elke finally looks him in the eye. "The girl you exchanged spinning wheels with, the child–woman you like me to bring you news about . . ." Sadness drains the color from her face. "Oh, my little man, she . . ."

The spinner's heart stops pumping; his lungs stop pulling in air. "Is she ill?"

"No. She is locked in a room in the castle."

The spinner breathes again. Saskia is not ill. She can be rescued. "Why is she locked up?"

"It's her father's fault, the wretched drunk. He told the king she could spin straw into gold."

The spinner staggers over to the spinning wheel. He holds on as though the wheel can keep him here, keep him whole. Sweat breaks out across his back. Spinning gold has been the curse of his life. Would that it not be hers. He hears himself say, "And can she?"

Elke gasps. "Of course not. The king won't abide false boasts. He locked her in a room full of straw, and if the straw is not gold in the morning, she dies."

"The miller said she could do it. You don't know for sure that she can't."

"The girl shouts from the room. She was shouting when I left. Begging for mercy. She's as harebrained as her father."

The spinner takes his two walking sticks from beside the door where they lean. "Can you get me into the locked room?"

Elke stands and reaches out her hands in protest. "Do you forget how far it is? And dusk will be upon us soon."

"Can you get me into her room?"

"If I'm caught . . ." Elke covers her mouth with one hand.

The spinner knows this is a king who uses death as punishment. He must persuade Elke carefully. But even as he opens his mouth to speak, she nods. Her eyes hold him as though he is a jewel. The spinner is flustered. But this is not the moment to ponder the look in Elke's eyes. "Let's go."

The spinner travels slowly. With each step he sways wildly, despite his walking sticks. And the path they make through the woods is confounded with roots and holes and rocks. The afternoon turns to evening and then to full night before they arrive at the castle.

The guards walking the perimeter loom large in the moonlight. But the spinner hobbles past them without hesitation. Elke's presence is enough. Indeed, the guards might well pay him no mind even if he were alone. No one bothers a cripple, so long as he's empty-handed.

They enter the main doors and follow corridors right and left. Elke stops in front of the last door.

"Come back in a half hour to let me out."

"Promise me once again that she'll still be in this room when the king comes in the morning."

"I promise."

"Tell me what you hope to accomplish." This demand has come in many forms since they left his shack.

The spinner still refuses to obey it.

Elke puts both hands under the heavy bolt and lifts.

The girl called Saskia sits on the stool, staring at nothing. She doesn't blink as the spinner closes the door behind him. Her hair glistens gold with moonlight. The spinner comes closer.

Saskia jumps off the stool with a start. Her mouth is an open ring. "Am I asleep?"

"No."

She licks her lips. "I dreamed. I dreamed of dying gently."

"Do you want to die?"

"No."

The spinner touches the wheel. It spins smoothly, this wheel he knows like his own skin.

And now Saskia seems to come to full awareness. "Who are you?"

The spinner looks at her face and sees her struggle to hide the horror she feels at the sight of him. He keeps his hand on the wheel. This is what he expected, after all. It will take time for her to get accustomed to him, time for her to look within him to his true self.

Saskia's hands go to the necklace she wears. She rubs the shells.

The spinner comes close.

Saskia stiffens, but she doesn't step backward. She sucks in air and doesn't release it.

The spinner looks closely at the necklace; it is the one he gave Saskia's mother. He stands so close now that he could touch the necklace with his lips if he let his head fall forward. Still she doesn't step back. He hears her burst of breath at long last; then another sharp intake; and, finally, the loud in-and-out rhythm of hope.

"How did you get in here?"

The spinner is surprised. Didn't she see him come through the door?

"Are you magic?"

The spinner recognizes it is to his advantage that she follow this line of thought. She is more likely to obey him if she believes he has extraordinary powers. He waits.

She whispers, "Are you good or evil?"

The spinner waits.

"Why . . ." Her voice is tremulous. "Oh, why are you here?"

He reaches a hand up and touches her cheek with his fingertips. It is cool from drying tears. "Why were you crying, miller's daughter?" My daughter, he thinks. My dear daughter.

"The king told me to spin this straw into gold. If I don't do it by morning, I die."

"Can you do it?"

"No."

"Why does the king think you can?"

"My father said I could."

"Why did the miller say that?"

"He boasts absurdities when he's been drinking."

"Still," says the spinner, "that's a strange boast."

"He says my mother told him of someone who could."

The spinner nods. So Saskia's mother, that young woman long ago, believed he spun the gold after all. He wonders what else she told her old husband about him.

Saskia puts her hands on the spinner's shoulders. Her eyes hold his.

Her act unravels him. The spinner wants to withdraw, away from this lovely face and all the loss it carries. But she needs his help. His own daughter needs his help.

He will do what he can. And then? He taps the center shell of her necklace, and longing for her mother transfixes him. "What will you give me if I spin this straw into gold?"

Saskia takes off the necklace and puts it over the spinner's head.

The spinner is enchanted: There is a certain rightness to her act, though he never could have anticipated it. He sits on the stool. He has not dared to question this moment. But now he takes both hands and slowly places the foot of his rumpled leg to the pedal. He has not used this leg since the last time he spun straw into gold—when he still loved her mother. It must work now. It must, for his daughter's life hangs in the balance. He holds his right hand out to Saskia. She gives him straw.

His hand shakes as the tears fall, soaking the straw.

He spins, every pump of his rumpled leg a prayer.

The air fills with angels that dance around Saskia.

Eighteen

THE king walks from one giant coil of gold to the next, brilliant in the morning sun. He clasps his hands behind at the waist. He moves his lips as though he's talking to himself. His servant stands in the doorway and gapes.

Saskia tries to see the gold through the king's eyes. He thinks he's witnessing magic.

And he is. Saskia knows spinning. She has experimented with the hair of every kind of animal she could get her hands upon—sheep, rabbit, horse, dog. She has experimented with every plant that suggests itself to her imagination, from grasses to vegetables to flowering bushes. Beauty comes from these animals and plants.

But what that spinner did last night went beyond beauty. Saskia shudders.

The king inspects the spinning wheel. He bends to consider the axle support. He tries to turn it. His obvious ignorance of spinning seems grotesque to Saskia. He rises and looks at her.

Saskia looks back at him.

The king continues to look. His gaze orders.

Saskia has only lies to offer. She doesn't speak.

"Is this a magic wheel?"

What might that mean? "If you call my yarns magic, then yes."

The king seems to like this answer. "Who are you?"

"The miller's daughter," says Saskia without hesitation. And now that the words are out, she can see how true they are. Every turn of her life so far has been caused by a lurch in Father's behavior.

"Are you a witch? A tool of evil?"

"No." Saskia's heart thumps denial. "No!"

"The miller said you were a wizard."

Saskia searches back over Father's words of yesterday. "A wizard with fibers."

The king's eyes cloud with doubt. "You've done well. Can you perform other miracles?"

"No."

The king ponders this. "But you admit that this is a miracle?"

"Yes. But I am no witch, I swear."

"That better be true, or I'll have you burned." His face reddens. "You make gold with a magic wheel." He laughs that greedy laugh she knows now. "I'll have another room filled with straw. A bigger room. And you will spin all of it into gold."

Saskia shakes her head. This cannot be happening. Not again. No.

"You shall," says the king, his voice rising.

Saskia remembers how Father's voice rose to exactly that same pitch when he wanted her to trade Mother's spinning wheel for the new one. In this moment, she realizes she hates Father.

"The room will be full of gold by morning. Or you will die. And this time, now that I know you're a wizard for true, this time the death won't be swift. No one disobeys the king."

Saskia eats her dinner in the second room of straw. She has examined this room just as thoroughly as the last one, of course.

She has kissed the spinning wheel on every part, mobile and stationary.

She has pumped the pedal with her usual leg, then with the other—fast, like last night's spinner.

She has touched every stalk of straw.

There is nothing left to do now. Either the contorted spinner will come again or he will not.

Her skin crawls at the memory of his uneven countenance, of his unnatural power. That man saved her.

Mysterious man. He cried as he spun. Maybe it hurt his rumpled leg. Yet he did it in exchange for a necklace of shells. A pittance.

There is no reason to expect him to return.

What method of slow death will the king devise?

Although this room is larger than the last, it must be located near the center of the castle, for it has no windows to look from. Saskia closes her eyes and looks within.

Dagmar and Saskia skip between rows of wheat, batting

at the insects that make their bare shoulders itch. They are five years old.

They exchange stone collections at eight years old. They swing and drop into the lake at ten. They spin side by side at eleven. They sell yarn together year in, year out.

Last month they shared dreams. Dagmar was fifteen already. She'll be wed soon. And Saskia won't be at the wedding of the only person she cares about.

Saskia cries now. She can't stop crying.

When she hears the bolt lifted from the door, she raises her chin from her chest in time for her eyes to meet the spinner's as he slips into the room. The door shuts behind him; the bolt clanks into place.

The spinner is more distorted of face, more lopsided and twisted of body than she remembered. But thanks be to everything good that he has come again.

"I didn't sleep," Saskia says, swallowing a sob. "I daydreamed of living gently."

The spinner hobbles to her with a slowness that complains of exhaustion and pain. She rises from the stool, and he takes her place. His head is now at the level of her chest. His spirit is palpable; it would cut a hole in her flesh and enter her heart. "Were they good dreams?" he asks quietly.

Saskia laces her fingers together in front of her bodice, as much to hold in the passions of those dreams as to make a barrier against this gnarled spinner, who pries into her heart so unexpectedly. She is already more vulnerable to him than she wants. Yet she finds herself answering openly: "It hurt to think of leaving them, of never having them again."

The spinner touches her cheeks with both hands at once,

wiping away the tears. "What will you give me, miller's daughter, oh, what can you offer, if I spin all this straw into gold?" Her eyes follow his hands as they lower past her own—past the ring on her finger.

Saskia looks carefully at the ring. Her ring finger is precisely over her heart. And now she sees: The twisted thread of gold is not a bird's nest, as she used to think of it. No. Mother's ring is a ball of gold yarn. "Could my mother spin straw into gold?"

The spinner doesn't speak. But Saskia sees the apple of his throat move dry, up and down. He knows the answer. He knew her mother. She realizes now that she suspected that somehow all along. He is crying. Silent.

She pulls the ring off her finger. With surprise, she finds the spinner's hands are large. She slides the ring onto his last finger and hears the sharp intake of his breath.

The spinner raises the ring toward his lips, but he does not kiss it. Instead, he holds out his hand. With both arms, Saskia gathers a bundle of straw. The spinner cries and spins. Gold thread hisses to the floor.

THE king stands stunned at the sight of so much gold. But he recovers more quickly this morning. "Dawn sparkles off gold becomingly." He rubs his hands together. "It is amazing indeed to have one's own wizard. I'll put you in a bigger room yet. More straw, more gold."

"No." Saskia's voice starts as a broken half whisper. This was exactly her fear, of course. "No," she says louder, her voice strengthened by desperation.

"How dare you say no to me!"

"Your greed has no natural end. What can you possibly do with all that gold? This has to stop." This has to stop before you kill me, she thinks. For even if the spinner should come to help her again, she has nothing to give him now—and the exchanges are an intrinsic part of their arrangement.

"No one speaks like that to me." The king's nostrils flare.

He opens his hands to the gold coils. "Have you done this before?"

"Never."

"Why not?"

Saskia breathes shallow and quick. "Have you ever seen gold before, Your Majesty?"

"I have goblets inlaid with gold. I have amulets. I have a gold hilt on my sword. I am your king."

"Have you ever seen yarn like the yarns I spin—yarns of violets and cotton, of rye and silk, of apple leaves and spiderweb? Have you?"

"No."

"Never, Your Majesty?"

"Never."

"Then why should I waste my time spinning gold, when I can make beauty no one has seen before?"

The king shakes his head. Then he stops, holds still. "Are you wise?"

"I'm a spinster, Your Majesty."

"You live alone with the drunken miller."

It is not a question. The king has made inquiries about her. Saskia waits.

"You've known hardship," the king says almost quietly. "You've barely scraped by."

From his tone, Saskia can guess where this is leading. But she doesn't want to be the king's spinster. Not after all this. At any moment he might put her before a bale of straw and demand gold. "I am content with my life, Your Majesty. I don't seek change."

"Indeed." The king absently twists the tip of his beard

into a tight point. "No commoner would stand before the king and not seek betterment." He looks Saskia in the eyes, and his face is gentle. "You're right. One more room will be enough. And once you've spun it, you'll be queen."

"Queen?" says Saskia, uncomprehending.

"And why not? You are beautiful. You are capable of miracles. You are wise. And there's no hint of greed in you. You are a commoner by birth, but not by form and spirit."

"No." Saskia's legs give way. She collapses to a squat and falls backward into a coil of gold. She hugs her knees.

The king reaches a hand under her chin and tilts her head up toward him. "It's easy for you. One final task. By morning, you shall spin all the straw in the third room into gold."

Easy for me? "And if I refuse?"

"Don't."

Saskia wakes. She is still in the third room, where the king's servant led her this morning. She is still hopeless. And night has fallen.

There is noise in the hall. Saskia's hands do a quick inventory, racing up and down her body, as they have done repeatedly since she was locked in this room. The finding is the same: There is nothing left to give the spinner. He will enter to greet an empty-handed woman. He will leave behind a dead woman.

Twenty

T H E spinner leans on Elke, hopping on his good foot. Everyone inside the castle should be asleep; still they will not take the chance of someone hearing the click of his walking sticks. They hardly breathe as they make their way awkwardly through the long corridor and, finally, down the stone stairs, down, down to the room of straw.

"How do you help her?" whispers Elke. She stops in front of the bolted door and hands him the walking sticks she had tucked under one arm. "Exactly how do you do it?"

"Does it matter?" The spinner leans on his sticks. The walk back and forth through the woods for two days in a row and now yet again wearies him. But this will be the last time. Elke told him that the king will either kill Saskia or marry her tomorrow. One more room of straw, one more room of gold, and that's the end. His daughter will not only be free of that stupid miller; she'll be rich. Tonight he will not call her "miller's daughter." Tonight he wins her safety forever.

"Does the girl do anything at all?" Frustration and fear tinge Elke's cheeks. "My little man, it's you who spins the gold, isn't it?" Her hands waver in front of her lips. "If the king should find out . . ."

The lost look in her eyes demands recognition; the risk she runs for him heightens each day her complicity continues. He pinches the cloth on her sleeve and pulls her toward him so that her face is but inches from his. "I'm grateful for everything you do."

For a tiny moment, Elke closes her eyes, as though she would swoon. She opens them, and all emotion is gone; her face sets into that of the businesslike headmistress of the servants that he met that fateful day in the market almost five years ago.

The spinner releases his fingers.

Elke lowers the bolt with effort and brushes off her hands. "Use caution."

The spinner opens the door.

Saskia is standing as he enters, her eyes clear, still. Her hands hang limp at her sides. Her neck, shoulders, chest, all relax into a dreadful softness. The spinner knows: His daughter has given up. "Didn't you think I'd come?"

"I knew you'd come." Her silty voice betrays the sadness. "Did you . . ." She clears her throat. "Did you, by any chance, owe my mother a favor?"

The spinner owed the young woman nothing. If anything, the debt goes in the opposite direction.

It's almost dawn already, the spinner took so much longer to struggle here this time. His body is as tremulous as his daughter's voice. And the job is huge. He must begin immediately.

Saskia lets out a quiet sigh, thin like a strand of silk.

The spinner hobbles to her and bends his head backward to look up into those hazel eyes. But now he sees her straight: small nose; smooth, hairless cheeks; delicate chiseled ears. The peaks of the upper lips are sharp, as is the point of the chin. The throat is long, slender, quivering. He straightens his own neck and lets his eyes wander over gently rounded breasts that stand high on the chest, narrow waist that closes over strong muscles, down to widening hips—promising hips. Heat emanates from this torso. Beneath the shift, he senses the outline of firm thighs. The air holds the scent of woman.

She turns slowly.

The spinner almost falls backward at the shock of her movement. But for the scent of her, the heat of her, he could have thought he stood before a statue.

Her back is to him now. She rotates her hips just barely, as though perhaps in her inexperience she only guesses at how women do this. The naïveté makes the move exquisitely seductive. She turns until she faces him once more. Unspilled tears render her eyes luminous. She touches the shell necklace that she gave him. She touches the ring that she gave him. Then she flutters her fingers down from her neck to her hips. "This is all I have left to give." Her voice catches. "Please. Accept the exchange."

So this is her assessment. As the awfulness of her desperate offer realizes itself in his soul, outrage burns. He is mortified and sickened that she thinks he wants her. The spinner would retch with shame if she were right.

His eyes bore into her. She is his daughter. Flesh of his flesh. They are bound to one another as intimately as life allows. He loves her. Love should come from her, as well. Surely love will come.

He puts a hand on her arm.

She blinks. He can see her jaw tighten. Her upper lip twitches. Her eyes flash—is it recognition? Recognition at last? Oh, oh, no—they flash revulsion. And now they glaze over, as she distances herself. Her body is here with the spinner, but her spirit has fled.

He gnashes his teeth in fury. She is her mother's daughter; she sees only with her eyes. He hates her. And she deserves it, unfeeling ingrate that she is. He will leave her here to die because she has nothing to give him. Nothing, nothing.

He wants nothing in this world but love.

Oh, God, the thought thunders—it would cause his skull to explode: There is something she can give him. It is a gift of her womanhood that he will trade for, a gift she doesn't merit having anyway; it is someone who will be raised in the spinner's home, someone who will look with heart as well as eyes.

The spinner lets his walking sticks drop. He puts both hands on Saskia's hips and squares her to him, his nose practically brushing her chin. The intimacy of his act sends shudders through her. Her tears fall hot on his cheeks. "Don't cry," he whispers, as much to himself as to her. "I offer you a trade." His hands clutch tight; his throat would choke. "Your life in exchange for another's."

Saskia's lips, which were slightly parted before, now come together. She wipes the tears away. "You speak riddles." She licks her lips. "Please explain."

"I will spin all this straw." The spinner waves one arm

around at the mounds and loses his balance. He grabs her hip again, holds as though he will collapse if he doesn't. "All of it, all the straw, into gold. I will save your life."

Saskia nods, her face expectant.

His throat burns now. A fire rages through his every part. "In exchange for your firstborn."

Saskia's face becomes a mask. The spinner listens to the echo of his own hideous words. He knows his request is unpardonable. Someone cries inside him.

No. This cannot be.

He repents. He will spin this straw for the girl. She is his daughter, she is, despite her feelings toward him. He will spin. His tears soak her bodice.

Yet he does not speak. The silence grows. He does not retract his offer. Oh, pitiless world, he cannot.

Saskia pries the spinner's fingers loose. She cups her hands around his shoulders and guides him to the spinning stool. She loads her arms with straw. "A life for a life," she says. "May God forgive us both."

PART FIVE

Preparation

Twenty-one

L E AV E us." The king looks at Saskia, but his words are directed to his servant. The servant goes out, closing the door behind him.

Saskia bends her arms, so that her forearms lie one on the other, her hands cupping her elbows, in front of her waist. She straightens her back and looks tall into the face of this king, working to keep her eyes from betraying her fear. The king believes her a wizard, after all. That is her only playing card.

"I offer you a lifetime of joy and leisure."

Saskia shakes her head.

The king steps toward her.

Saskia holds her ground. "I will not marry you."

A ruddy hue creeps up the king's neck and cheeks. "No one refuses me."

Saskia's eyes see dancing points of light. If she refuses,

she dies now. If she marries, the day will come when the king will want more gold, and she'll die then. An irrelevant memory comes: "In one week I will be fifteen."

The king seems confused, wary. "A birthday makes a good wedding day. A bad death day."

Birthday, death day. Saskia is already as good as dead. The realization frees her tongue. "Are you a stupid man?"

The king opens his mouth, then snaps it shut. A muscle by his right eye spasms. "It would appear you are not so wise after all."

"Do you forget the last three days? Each morning you slated my death; each night I suffered under this threat." Saskia's voice is soft; her rage lies curled like a drowsy lynx. She turns in a circle slowly, her hands outstretched toward the walls, until she faces the king again. "The third room was as large as this one. I squeezed myself between the straw and the walls and measured. Thirty of my paces by twenty of my paces. Thirty by twenty. Thirty by twenty. Over and over and over. Nothing but straw. Thirty by twenty. Straw."

"Straw and your spinning wheel. You had the means!"

"A savage threat."

"You did it. You spun it into gold. What did a threat matter when you knew you could do the task?" The king reaches for her hands.

Saskia holds her own elbows tight and stretches herself even taller. "You didn't know if I could. You left me that first night thinking that in the morning you would kill me." As I thought you would.

The red in the king's cheeks now crosses the bridge of his nose. "Your father said you could do it. How was I . . ."

"... to believe a drunk?" Saskia's voice hardens. "We are neither of us stupid, Your Majesty. We both know you prepared to kill me that first night." She takes a deep breath. "I will not marry a man who would kill me for failing to spin straw into gold and who would make me queen for succeeding."

The king takes her by the forearms. "I've told you there are more reasons than that for my wanting you." His voice is thick, like feathers in a quilt. It could suffocate.

"Let me go."

"Go then," says the king suddenly. He sweeps his hand toward the door. "Go back to your world. See how it shrinks." He leaves.

Saskia stares at the doorway. She is free. Just like that, the nightmare is over. She puts both hands on the table to steady herself until the nausea passes. Then she runs, before the king changes his mind.

Twenty-Two

R O B I N S fly through the bushes. People sell apples and swine flesh. Saskia is aware of these things, but only vaguely. She is beyond the market now. Hoofbeats from behind startle her. She can feel the hands, the ropes, the imprisonment already. She runs, falls, opens her mouth to scream. But the horse goes on by.

No one follows Saskia. There is no flood pursuing her. In fact, it is dry for a spring day.

After a long while, she spies Father at the road's edge. He waves. He's expecting her. How did he know?

Saskia has not spoken with Father since his fateful boast. Her jaw clenches.

The wagon stands outside the barn with their horse hitched to it. Where is Father planning on going?

Father rushes to her. His eyes sparkle. She sniffs the air; he has not been drinking. So his energy is unexplained. He puts one arm around her waist. Saskia recoils, but he holds her fast and ushers her homeward. "You came back to me. I knew you would. When I heard, I knew."

His breathless enthusiasm confuses Saskia. "What did you hear, Father?"

"Everything. He would have stolen you from me. But you didn't go."

Stolen me from you? thinks Saskia. Is this the man who put my life in jeopardy?

Father laughs, his face full to the sky in joy. "You didn't go. You're still mine," he crows and sprints ahead. He opens the door with a bow.

Saskia steps inside cautiously.

The room is full of straw. Floor to ceiling. In the corners. Blocking the window. Everywhere.

Her spinning wheel sits in the middle.

Saskia is rooted to the spot. "How did my spinning wheel get here?"

"The king's messenger brought it."

"When?" Her voice cracks on the single word.

"Not long ago. An hour and a half, maybe. Long enough for me to fetch the straw. I only just finished unloading the wagon." Father brushes off the stool with his hand. "Are you ready to make us rich?"

"No."

"What? Are you tired? If you need to rest before you spin . . ."

"I'll never spin that straw into gold."

"Don't be insolent, daughter."

Daughter, again. His voice is so far away, she can hardly hear it now. "I won't."

"You will do as I say."

Saskia almost says she can't. But Father isn't to be trusted with that knowledge. "You would have got me killed. I owe you nothing."

"I raised you. I . . ."

"How dare you say that!" she screams.

"Watch how you speak to your father!"

Dagmar's brother, Stefan, the one who is but a year older than the girls, rides past on the road. He calls out, "Dagmar sends greetings." He hesitates, then rides on.

Saskia is disoriented for a moment. Stefan has never come delivering messages before. But, yes, this is lucky. Dagmar's message strengthens her. "I'm not yours," she says, speaking softly once again.

"What?"

"When you met me on the road, you said I was still yours. But I'm not." She takes one last look at the straw. "I hope you paid so much for this straw that you can't afford to get drunk for months." She goes out to the road and walks toward Dagmar's home.

"Saskia! What's the matter with you? All I want is gold. For us. You and me. You made the king richer, and look how much he had already. Make us rich." Father grabs at Saskia's elbow and spins her around to face him.

"Good-bye, miller."

"I am your father. Show respect."

Saskia pulls her arm free and runs. The powder of the dry road billows up. Her heart gallops. So loud. So loud.

But it is Stefan's horse, not her heart, after all. Stefan alights beside her and puts out his cupped hands. Saskia uses them to jump to the horse's back. Stefan mounts behind her.

All is done without a word.

Saskia collapses onto the horse's neck, clutching to keep from slipping beneath those hooves. But she can't help looking back for an instant. Father has gone inside. It has never taken him long to give up.

So two men have relinquished her this day.

Saskia feels lost. Falling.

Her mind frantically seeks a foothold.

By the time they arrive at the house, Saskia has a plan. She will offer herself as personal spinster and maid to Dagmar and her new husband in exchange for shelter.

Saskia jumps to the ground.

Dagmar's mother rushes to greet her. "Welcome." She leads Saskia into the house.

"Where is Dagmar?"

"Taking count of the new lambs. She'll be back to eat soon."

"I'll go find her."

"Stay a moment, Saskia. Sit at the table with Stefan while I get you an apple tart."

Stefan paces the house now. His behavior matches Saskia's feelings. And Dagmar's mother has never before told Saskia to sit while she served her. "I'll help Dagmar." Saskia goes quickly out the door before anyone can protest.

There's Dagmar now. Saskia runs to her.

Dagmar looks up.

They hug, holding long.

Saskia wipes at her tears with the back of her hands. "My father . . . he filled the house with straw."

"I guessed as much." Dagmar's hands move up and down

Saskia's back, keeping her in their circle. "Mother saw him pass with the wagon piled high."

So Dagmar, too, knows about the doings in the castle. Saskia steps back. "Does everyone think . . ." She licks her lips. Who can be trusted? "Did everyone hear I spun straw into gold?"

"It's all anyone can talk about." Dagmar looks Saskia in the eyes, and her face seeks an answer. "People are afraid."

"Of what?"

"They say you must be a witch."

"So that's why your mother acted so strange."

Dagmar gives a harrumph. "Mother has hopes. She wants Stefan to marry you."

Saskia shakes her head in disbelief. But then, oh, no, it all makes sense. "So I can make your family rich."

"Everyone wants a better life, Saskia."

"Do you, too, see me as a source of riches?"

"I see my best friend."

A ewe pushes her tough muzzle, her spongy lips, into Saskia's palm. "How many lambs are there?"

Dagmar sighs. "Twenty-three." She looks across the scattered flock. "How did you do it?" she asks so softly Saskia at first thinks she imagined it.

"I can't tell you."

Dagmar nods. "Was it hard?"

"Yes. Don't try it. I'm not a witch, Dagmar."

"I didn't think you were."

"Everyone in town, everyone I meet, will either be afraid of me or want me to spin gold for them, or both."

Dagmar looks away.

Saskia's sense of falling returns, but now there are no more footholds.

"Where will you go?" whispers Dagmar.

Saskia heads south, away from the castle. She will beg a ride with the first wagon that passes, wherever it's going. Then she'll beg another ride. And another. She'll go until she's sure no one will have heard of the girl who can spin straw into gold.

Too soon she hears hoofbeats. A group of them. Saskia senses who it is without looking over her shoulder.

The three accompanying servants on horseback encircle her. The king dismounts and blocks her path. "You will make a worthy queen."

"I will not marry you."

"And what would you do instead? Spin straw into gold for your drunken father? For a drunken husband, perhaps?"

He's had someone spy on her all morning. Or maybe he just guessed how fast her world would shrink—he's not the idiot her father is. "I spin wool and linen and cotton," says Saskia, amazed at the false conviction in her voice. "I will find employment."

"I will treat you well, Saskia." He takes her by the forearms, as he did in the castle this morning. "I promise."

"Ah." Saskia lets her head fall back, her whole body teeter within his hands. "What about the next time the greed for riches claws at your chest? Will you fill the castle ballroom with straw?"

"I told you that was the last time."

She collects her strength and stands firm once more.

"You don't want me. You want someone to sit at the wheel that spins straw into gold."

"Stubborn woman! No one challenges my word." The king grabs her around the waist and half hurls her onto his horse. He mounts behind her in a flash, holding her fast with one arm. "Bring her magic spinning wheel back to the castle," he barks to his servants. "Fast!"

"No," screams Saskia. But her scream is lost in the hoof-beats as they gallop the road back to the castle. Yet another trial, and this time the king will witness her failure. She closes her eyes against the sting of the wind and sees stacks of straw rising to the skies, all of it tumbling onto her, smothering her.

They are already within the outer walls. A servant rushes to take charge of the horse.

The king jumps down, dragging Saskia after him.

Saskia lets herself be pulled like a dead sheep. Worse, for she feels her physical self disperse; she is empty as a bloody fleece. Powerless.

The king shouts at another servant. Something about wood. He yanks Saskia this way and that in a crazy, torturous path across the castle. She stumbles after him. They go outside, past the purples and pinks of early spring flowers. They enter a walled-in courtyard.

Two men prepare a bonfire.

A sob breaks from Saskia's chest. Death by fire. When she fails the trial, she will endure the cruelest method of death.

A servant carries her spinning wheel and stands it beside the woodpile. How did they get it here so fast? Everything happens so fast. She rushes to the wheel and clasps it, her only reliable means of both sustenance and beauty. This wheel has been her salvation. It's so unfair that it should bring about her ruin now. Unfair, unfair. She holds so tight her knuckles go white.

The king grabs at the wheel. But Saskia holds on tight. And now she realizes there will be no test. She's to be burned immediately. The king believes the wheel is magic. As long as he has the wheel, he doesn't need her. But, oh, as long as she holds tight to the wheel, he will not kill her.

"You'll see," says the king. "You'll see."

Wild-eyed, Saskia sees nothing. "Straw," she screams.

"Yes!" The king lets go of the wheel and grabs Saskia tight. "Bring straw!" he shouts to the men.

Saskia can't stop screaming.

"Set it all on fire," shouts the king.

Flames shoot up from the mountain of straw.

"Watch," the king says in Saskia's ear. He pushes her aside now and yanks the wheel away.

Saskia sees her spinning wheel thrown through the air into the flames. Her wheel. He has burned her wheel, not her. Her beloved wheel. It is as though he burns her soul.

"The magic wheel is gone. You can never spin straw into gold again." And the king is holding her, stroking her hair. "I want you, Saskia. And I'll have you."

Twenty-three

SASKIA massages the king's arms and shoulders. He is a difficult man—intemperate and impatient. Still, Saskia has learned ways to calm him. She rolls to her side and feigns sleep.

The king rises, finally. Saskia keeps her eyes lightly closed. She discerns his outline through her lashes. He goes to the dressing room, where he is met by his waiting servant, Ludwig.

She slides out of bed quietly and crosses the stone floor to her own dressing room, on the opposite side of this huge bedroom. She goes to the urn in the corner. Bridget has filled it with fresh water, like always. Saskia splashes her face, then waters the potted plants that make this room junglelike. Bridget blinked with surprise when Saskia asked for the first two camelia bushes. She exclaimed at the request for another six. But she quickly swallowed her exclamation. To her, Saskia is the queen who did the impossible, spun straw into gold. Her powers are not to be underestimated or her desires questioned.

Saskia empties every drop of the water over the roots of those bushes. Then she reaches behind the chest, where she has tucked the bottle. She pours the full bottle of vinegar into the urn. She squats over it and washes herself inside and out. Nothing grows in vinegar. Nothing will take root inside her. She thinks always about her promise to the contorted spinner. But as long as she rinses with vinegar, she will never see him again.

A sad laugh escapes her throat. Oh, she will see that spinner again. He haunts her dreams.

She lifts the urn and carefully pours the soiled vinegar back into the bottle. Then she relieves herself into the waste bucket and dresses.

This is another unexpected request—that she be allowed to dress herself. Bridget hasn't yet fully accepted that idea. She comments on it often, sometimes only with her eyes.

Saskia holds the vinegar bottle hidden in a fold of her skirt and goes down the stairs to the kitchen. The cook, Angelika, rises in greeting, then quickly sits again at the table, where she shells peas. Unlike Bridget, she adapts without hesitation to Saskia's habits. She has never questioned Saskia about the bottle that she empties into the slop for the pigs. She doesn't even watch anymore as Saskia kneels beside the vinegar barrel and refills the bottle.

A squeal comes from outside the kitchen door. Saskia peeks. A piglet runs along the wall. Somehow he has wandered so far from the sow that he cannot find his way back.

Saskia looks around. The kitchen yard is empty. She sets her bottle of vinegar by the door and reaches for the piggy. It proves remarkably hard to catch. She chases after it, eventually steering it to the sty.

Saskia laughs and hurries back to the kitchen.

Bridget stands at the open door, holding the bottle of vinegar.

Saskia shivers. Goose bumps cover her. She snatches the bottle from Bridget and looks directly into her questioning eyes. She takes a swig, rinses it around her teeth, spits it onto the ground. Then she brushes past Bridget without meeting her eyes.

She tucks the bottle into the folds of her skirts as she climbs the stairs. Will Bridget believe she uses vinegar only to keep her mouth clean? She should have swallowed it. After all, people drink vinegar whenever they fear they might have eaten something rancid. Saskia didn't think fast enough.

She hates deception. Yet deception coats her every relationship in this castle. No one knows the queen did not spin straw into gold. No one knows the queen works at staying barren. The king would have her killed for either transgression.

Fear curls Saskia's innards. But she has lived with danger before—that long year when Father was continually drunk. She survived then.

She hides the vinegar bottle behind the chest. Will there be enough left in it to clean her out thoroughly tomorrow? She goes back downstairs and out to the courtyard.

Ludwig talks with the king. At Saskia's approach, the servant leaves.

Saskia feels heat climb her neck to her cheeks. Do the servants talk about her? This king tolerates nothing suspect. "My Lordship." She touches the king's beard softly. A memory comes—and, oh, what better way to show she's trustworthy? "May I shave you?"

"An unusual request." He raises an eyebrow. "Why?"

"I've lived with you for three months, and I don't know what lies under that beard. I long to see."

One side of his mouth lifts in a bemused smile. "You want to shave me now?" His hand sweeps backward toward the table laden with breads and cheeses and meats. "Breakfast waits."

"And it can keep waiting."

The king takes Saskia's hand and leads her inside. "Bring a razor," he calls to a servant. They go upstairs to his washroom. He sits in the chair he always sits in for grooming.

Saskia picks up the scissors from the side table. She cuts the king's beard close.

Ludwig appears, razor in hand. "Your Majesty?"

"Give the queen the razor. And you are excused."

Ludwig looks quickly at Saskia. His eyes are doubtful.

Saskia puts the scissors down. She steps forward and takes the razor confidently. "Thank you."

"Of course, Your Highness." Ludwig leaves.

Saskia places the razor on the table. She finds the bar of soap and lathers the short, stiff bristles that remain. Then she takes up the razor. She quells her trepidations, willing her hand to be as steady as Dagmar's was the night they shaved the miller.

The razor reveals a square jaw, high, wide cheeks.

"You are comely," Saskia says, stepping back and looking at him with wonder. She hands him a mirror.

He looks long at himself. Then he smiles at Saskia.

He trusted her with a razor. The possible reasons why are as numerous as the reasons why she didn't slit his throat. Still, she wishes he trusted her out of affection. He's young for a king. Somewhere inside him, there must be a need for love. And love offers the best protection if her deceptions are ever revealed.

They go down the stairs and out to the courtyard to eat.

"I'm leaving for two nights," says the king.

Saskia feels a twinge—of what? She won't miss him. But the fact is that she'll have nothing to do while he's gone. "Take good care," she says. She butters a rich, sweet black roll. "I want a tutor, so I can learn to read. I want to start immediately."

The king takes a bite of wurst and looks up. "You're full of surprises today." He touches his own chin gingerly. The newly exposed skin is pale in the summer light.

"You said once that I was wise. A wise person should read."

"A wise man, perhaps."

"I ran a spinning business for years. I have a mind for business."

"What has this to do with reading?"

"If I could read, I could help in managing the castle's affairs," says Saskia. "I could keep the ledgers."

"You'll be raising children soon." The king reaches for a sweet bread. "They'll fill your time."

"Children play. Children sleep. They don't take every

waking moment." Saskia drinks her ale. "A lot goes into managing the castle affairs. Your time is too valuable to waste on details. A woman has a mind for details."

The king sits back and considers her. He strokes his chin again. At last he says, "All right." He stands.

Saskia stands, too. She can't keep the smile from her face. "Thank you."

The king takes her into his arms brusquely and kisses her. "I'll be back soon." He tilts his head. "I'll tell Ludwig to seek a tutor. When I return, you can begin lessons." He leaves.

Saskia watches his long stride, the bounce of his curling hair. The only person in this castle who cares in the least about her is walking away. For an instant, she glimpses the solitude of the years that spread before her.

When Bridget comes to gather the remains of the meal, Saskia speaks firmly. "There's a girl in town named Dagmar. She's the new wife of the baker Rudolph. Send an escort to bring her here."

Bridget nods and leaves.

The garden comes to life slowly, pinching at the edges of her awareness. The sky is deep blue today; the clouds invite her to stay outside; the birds sing.

Saskia kneels in the garden and clears dead leaves away from pale green shoots that struggle to thrive. She works at length, concentrating on plucking away unwanted wild plants, nurturing only those that will flower.

She thinks of Dagmar's wedding—her only excursion outside the castle since she came to live here. People she had known all her life gave wide berth to the queen who performed miracles. She hovered at the fringes of the celebration, fascinated by the glow of desire on Dagmar's cheeks, by the sensual energy radiating from Rudolph.

Dagmar married for love; Saskia married for survival.

The sun slowly warms the back of her neck, bringing a heavy calm. Her right hand is covered with damp dirt, but her left is clean. With that one hand, she twists her hair clumsily into a high knot.

Now other hands are in her hair, expert hands, undoing the knot, twisting tighter, retying it firmly.

Saskia turns and embraces Dagmar. "Thank you for coming."

"Who wouldn't come when the queen calls?"

"The queen didn't call you—I did."

"What's the difference?"

Saskia takes Dagmar's right hand. "I'm your friend."

The lines of Dagmar's face soften instantly. She closes her left hand over Saskia's. "And I'm yours. Is something wrong?"

Saskia bites her bottom lip. "I miss you."

"I miss you, too. But I have to get back to the bakery soon." Dagmar shrugs her shoulders. "Your life isn't work anymore. But mine is."

"Stay all day. I'll buy whatever Rudolph bakes at the price he normally gets for what you both bake together."

Dagmar blinks. "Well, all right. I could use a bit of a break," she says wistfully.

"Yes." Saskia's voice grows loud as the thought comes clear to her. "We'll make you the royal bakers, you and Rudolph. Then you can spend day after day with me."

Dagmar's smile comes slow, but genuine. "That would be good. That would be wonderful, Saskia."

"We'll buy everything from you at high prices." Excitement speeds Saskia's words.

Dagmar laughs. "You're daft. What would the king say?"

"He won't care. Plus I'll be managing the books soon."

Dagmar shakes her head with a wry smile. "You always make things turn out right."

Saskia bites her tongue. "Come." She leads the way in through the meeting hall to the stairway down. She stands at the top for a moment, her hand on the railing.

Dagmar moves closer. "Why do you hesitate?"

"I haven't been down there since he locked me in those rooms, three rooms, with straw. I thought I was dead."

Dagmar slides one arm around Saskia's waist. "I thought so, too, when the miller came back that first day. I cried all night. But then you did it. You spun the gold."

"Under threat of death each time."

Dagmar's arm tightens. "Let's not go down, Saski."

"I need to. I've wanted to find something since I first got here."

Dagmar's closed mouth works, as it does when she's chewing on the inside of her cheek in worry. "What?"

"My mother's spinning wheel."

"Oh." Dagmar sighs with relief. "Oh, that's right. The woman who traded wheels with you worked for the king. But why don't you just ask that woman?"

Saskia shakes her head. "I can't let anyone here think I might spin again. I'll never spin again. I just want to see something familiar—to know something from my old life is near." She runs down the stairs as she talks.

The room at the foot of the stairs is where Saskia spent her first night. It has been swept clean, but the air is still full of golden bits of straw dust that float in the sun rays from the high window. They burn Saskia's eyes; they invade her nose. Straw surrounds her again. She cannot breathe. Coughs shake her body.

Dagmar pulls her from the room. "Let's go back upstairs. You . . ."

"No." Saskia pulls herself free and opens the door to the next room. It is the slightly larger room of her second night. Equally empty but for the shimmering air. The room dims, and Saskia knows it will fill with straw, and the air will grow dense. She staggers to the hall.

They stand now outside the third door. Saskia touches the bolt that leans against the wall.

"Were you locked in here, too?" Dagmar whispers.

"Yes."

Dagmar pulls Saskia's hand back from the bolt. She hugs Saskia. "Let's not look any further."

"Dagmar?" Saskia runs her hands on Dagmar's face as though she tries to learn her features with blind fingers.

"What, Saskia?"

"Will you have children?"

"Of course."

"If I find my mother's spinning wheel, will you teach your daughters to spin on it?"

"Of course."

Saskia kisses her friend on the cheek and cries.

Twenty-four

ELKE holds his newest skein to her cheek. "So soft. The queen will be delighted when I tell her you've spun this just for her."

The spinner steps back. "You must never mention me to her."

"And why not?"

"If you do, that would kill me."

Elke puts one hand over her mouth in horror.

The spinner didn't plan his words, and he doesn't know if they are true. All he knows is that the queen, his daughter, has made a promise that she undoubtedly regrets. She will try to find a way to break it. He has to stay away from her until the fateful moment when he takes his grandchild home. "Promise you'll never speak of me to her."

"I would never do anything to harm you." Elke sways toward him. "Will I never know what you did with her those three nights? Will you always be so mysterious, my little man?"

The intensity of her posture, the way her hands curl unconsciously so that her fingers pinch the folds of her skirt, the slight warming of her voice as she calls him her man, all reveal her longing. The spinner finally comprehends. This is no delusion born of misguided hopes. It is real. And it would be easy to reciprocate. But what is the love of this woman in comparison to the love of a child? A child he can hold in his hands and sing lullabies to. A child who will never see him as ugly. "What is it you love about me, Elke?"

Elke blinks away the glaze of romance. "Why, your yarns, of course. You are a master."

"Then collect them."

Elke takes the yarns, all of them, keeping her face turned from him.

After she has gone, the spinner stands a moment, overcome with the choice he has just made. A few weeks ago, he might have wept with joy at Elke's feelings for him.

The spinner picks up the heavy ax and straps it to his back so that his hands are free to use the walking sticks. He hobbles to the plane tree, takes the ax from his back, and swings. The ax cuts a tiny wedge from the bark and bounces to the ground. He picks it up and swings again. It smacks the bark at a strange angle and flies back at him, the butt knocking him in the chest. He falls backward. He swings the ax a third time. The head buries itself in the wood.

He collapses in a heap, then stretches onto his spine. His mind follows the air in through his nose, down his throat, into his lungs; and everything about the path is torturous, everything is wrong, all because of that leg that even now tenses, ready to pedal.

Both skinny arms reach straight up to the heavens. They bend and straighten and bend and straighten, pitiful sticks that can hardly bear their own weight. He rolls onto his stomach. The dirt is pungent with mushrooms. He pushes himself up on his arms. Then lets himself drop.

He stands and carefully cleans the dirt from the shells in the necklace he always wears. Dirt outlines the winding thread of his gold ring, too. He polishes it with the hem of his shirt. Then he searches for the right-sized rock. It sits not far from the base of the tree. His large hands cup it so completely, its color shows only between his fingers. He leans against a tree, and with his right hand he lifts the rock toward the heavens five times. Then he does the same with his left hand. He will do this every day. A little more every day, in fact. He will get strong and ready for this small person.

He cradles the rock in his arms and croons to it:

> The sky goes by goes sigh goes high
> It lifts your wings, it helps you fly
> You'll grow so wide and strong and long
> Like I once was, like I will be
> My sweet, my love, my one baby.

Twenty-five

SASKIA retches into the large pottery bowl beside the bed, put there expressly for her vomit.

Dagmar laughs and hands her a cup of sweet water.

"How can you laugh at my discomfort?" Saskia rinses her mouth and spits into the bowl.

"It won't last. Another few weeks at most." Dagmar bounces Franz on her knees. The baby gurgles. Dagmar smiles. "And it's for a good cause. After the whole long year and more that you had to wait before you found yourself with child, I'd think you'd rejoice at these heaves."

Saskia is horrified at these heaves, the harbinger of a loss too brutal to contemplate. She retches again, though her stomach is now empty.

She puts a hand on Franz's cheek. Wet with drool. Warm, alive, vulnerable, wonderful. He kicks both legs happily and looks at her with adoration.

Saskia stands and goes to the window. Summer covers the garden in bright yellow coreopsis flowers. A little fog lingers over the grounds. It will be a hot day. "Go on downstairs. I'll have breakfast with you as soon as I'm dressed."

"You know I already ate when I got up with Franz. I can't keep eating two breakfasts, Saskia, or I'll look like the pregnant one faster than you." Dagmar swings Franz around so that he straddles her hip. "Your belly begins to stick out a bit."

Saskia looks down in dismay at the middle of her white night shift. Her too-tender breasts stand out fuller than before; her tight abdomen curves softly under them.

"You can't keep it secret much longer, Saskia. And I don't understand why you want to." Dagmar comes over and kisses Saskia on the cheek. "I'll go bathe Franz while you eat." She leaves, singing to Franz as she goes.

Saskia looks out the window again. A wagon comes from afar on the south road, the road that leads to the mill. It can't be Father, for this wagon is drawn by an ox, not by the horse Father loves. Saskia realizes she thinks of him as Father again, not the miller. She doesn't miss him in the least. But ever since she found herself pregnant, she's had family on her mind. She grew up without her mother. The baby within her will grow up without either mother or father.

Saskia pulls the bell cord by her bed.

Bridget comes at a run, her small feet pattering on the stone staircase. She appears in the doorway, face flushed. "Yes, Your Highness."

"Send a runner to check on the miller."

"The miller?"

"My father."

Bridget's eyes widen. "Shall he be brought here?"

"No. I want him observed, nothing more." I want to know that he eats and sleeps and makes a living, thinks Saskia. I want to know that it's all right for me to forget him.

Bridget wrinkles her nose. "May I take away the bowl, Your Highness?" She walks quickly over, a small smile playing at the corners of her mouth. "It appears something disagrees with you every morning."

Saskia doesn't answer. She could swear Bridget to secrecy, but Dagmar's right: It wouldn't matter. Her belly rounds. The secret can't keep.

Her belly rounds.

Bridget takes the bowl and leaves.

The secret can't keep.

The king will know.

Saskia thinks of the softness of Dagmar's face when she looks at Franz. About her calm as the milk flows from her breasts into his round, round mouth. He has brought both of them happiness. Saskia can feel his fingers curl around hers, can see his toothless grin.

And now a baby grows within her.

But this birth can give her nothing but misery.

She walks across the room and looks out the north window. A man hobbles on two sticks through the courtyard beyond the wall. Her heart stops. But now she sees he has only one leg. And he's of normal height.

It is easy to pick the one-legged man out from the others, even at this distance, just by his gait.

So easy.

Saskia runs to the bell cord by her bed. She rings furiously.

Bridget appears. "Yes, Your Highness?"

"Fetch me the captain of the guards. Hurry, Bridget. And fetch the headmistress of the servants as well. I'll receive them in the meeting hall. Hurry."

Bridget's eyes go wide with alarm. "Yes, Your Highness." She runs off.

Saskia puts one finger in the little well at the base of her throat. She remembers the shallow indentation in the threading hook of her mother's spinning wheel. She strokes her skin rapidly.

Saskia's royal cape covers her shoulders, emphasizing the importance of the matter. She paces before Adolf and Elke. "There is a certain decrepit man, a spinner, actually, who lives in our kingdom."

Adolf and Elke look at her, eyes intent.

"If anyone sees him near the castle, I must be told immediately."

Adolf nods. "Are we to bring him to you?"

Saskia touches her own lips. "No, just tell me."

Elke holds her hands in front of her, clasped together. She looks as if she would speak. She turns to leave.

"Wait. Adolf, you may leave. Elke, stay."

Adolf backs out of the room.

Elke curtsies. "Your Highness?"

"You wanted to say something, Elke. What is it?"

Elke's eyes flicker away and back. "I was wondering about

Your Highness's health." She looks briefly at Saskia's middle, then back at her face.

"Your guess is right, Elke. But I wish to tell the king before you tell the servants."

Elke nods. "You have my warmest congratulations, Your Highness."

Warmest congratulations. Saskia wants to smile as freely as those words were spoken. And she would, but for the wretched spinner.

Twenty-six

JUST one more peg. The spinner pounds evenly, with little effort. He smiles. The shutter for the west window now hangs perfectly. He moves backward several meters and surveys the shack. All three windows in his home have shutters now. He tucks his hammer into the loop of his belt and swings himself between crutches along the path and in through the door.

The room feels warm from the luster of the dark cherry wood of this table. The spinner runs his hands along the surface with pride. He presses down; the table doesn't wobble one bit. The spinner didn't make the table himself. His carpentry skills improve with each project, but a table was the one piece of furniture he didn't dare to attempt. An eating table is too important; it serves to bind a family. The spinner thinks back to his brief stay with the boy Thomas and his father Hansjakob a full six years ago now. He loved eating across from them at the same table. For that short while, he could believe that he was part of a family. He could fool himself. But he won't have to fool himself when his grandchild comes to live with him. They will eat together at this most wonderful table. They will be family.

The spinner saws a slice of moist black bread from the loaf. The rock oven he built into the bottom of the fireplace works well, but next time he'll add more molasses to the dough. Children like breads sweet. And he'll twist the dough into the shapes of birds and fish. His grandchild's delighted laughter rings in his ears.

The spinner grabs his crutches and swings himself out to the clearing in front of his shack. He lies on his belly on the ground. Then he pushes himself up on his arms, lowers himself and pushes up again. He does this until the blood throbs in his temples. He loses count at fifty.

Now he rolls onto his back. The sky is clear blue with fluffy clouds. He reaches both arms toward those clouds, a daily ritual. The muscles stand out strong. His back and stomach and chest are strong, too, as is his one good leg. By the time this child is born, the spinner will be ready.

And the shack will be ready. It looks more like a real home each day. He built a bed, then shelves, the blanket chest, and finally, the clothes closet. And he had Elke buy the table for him and have it delivered to a drop-off point at the edge of the woods. Then they struggled to carry it to his shack. He couldn't do it by himself, and he couldn't risk having it delivered all the way. So he had to wait for her to come each day and help. It took them the better part of a week to get it all the way home.

It was worth it. He thinks of his grandchild tapping tiny

hands happily on the table, eating and talking and laughing.

Waiting for the grandchild was hard at first. When Elke would arrive saying there was no news yet, he'd fall into a gloom. Last summer went by painfully slowly for him. But when autumn came and the queen was still not pregnant, the spinner realized the wait was an opportunity for more than just strengthening his body and making the shack into a home. Since then, after his daily exercises and chores, he whittled. He started with something simple—a fish. Then he worked on the shapes of the animals he spied at night as he sat in the clearing. The basket in the corner now holds four wooden toys, hidden under a blanket: that first fish, a rabbit, an owl, a fox. The newest block of wood lies on the floor. A lynx will creep from it one day.

The spinner gets up now and goes to the queen's mother's spinning wheel. Elke buys as much yarn as he can spin. And since he'll be wanting all sorts of foods once the baby comes—fruits imported from hot countries and what else? Candies—children love candies—and, well, anything the child wants—since he'll need money to buy those things, he must spin as much as he can.

He has thought of spinning straw into gold again. That would make him rich fast. But perhaps that trick can be played only on that one special spinning wheel. He doesn't know because he's never tried on this one. But even if the trick lies within the spinner himself, he is loathe to try it, for the cost each time is so high. The first time the spinner spun straw into gold, he did it for himself. It cost his leg, his looks, and his health. The second time, he did it for Saskia. It will cost her firstborn.

Miracles cost.

The toll to the spinner the first time around wasn't worth it; the young woman married the miller anyway.

Will the toll to Saskia this second time be worth it?

The spinner can't think this way. He cannot afford to feel sympathy. Saskia is young and strong. She'll have other children. And she's the queen—she'll have whatever she desires. He's the one who needs now. He's the one who waits empty for the child to fill his life.

And anyway, he saved Saskia's life, and she didn't even love him for it. The first time he spun straw into gold, he counted on the young woman's love, and she was false in the end. He will not allow the second spinning of straw into gold to go loveless. His daughter owes him her child; she owes him someone who will love him.

"Hello, my little man." Elke stands in the doorway. She enters and puts the sack of wool in the corner and the sack of food on the table. This she does at least every other day. She's become a welcome fixture in his life, not just for the work and supplies, but for her company. How it happened he doesn't really know. But somehow after that moment in which she revealed herself to him, they moved ahead together, knowing they had to find an accommodation. He waits for her to take her usual seat.

Now, however, she changes the ritual. She clasps her hands behind her bottom and holds her lips closed in a thin line. He knows immediately that she bears news. Still, her face doesn't tell whether the news is good or bad.

"What is it?"

"Two things. One that troubles me and one that gives me joy."

"And both concern me?"

Elke nods. "They seem to."

"Speak. The joyful one first, please."

Elke pulls the bench close to the spinning stool that the spinner sits on. She settles herself with a flourish of her hands, all to emphasize the importance of her coming words. "The queen expects a baby."

The spinner clutches the wheel with one hand. For a moment he is dizzy. Finally. His grandchild.

Elke watches him intently. "Why do you care so much?"

The spinner closes his eyes and presses the heels of his palms against them to stem the flow of tears. He can't allow himself to make too much of a scene, to savor this news too long. When he feels in control of himself, he lowers his hands.

"I knew you would be overcome. I knew it." Elke's eyes hold him fast. "What happened between the two of you?" She leans forward.

"Nothing." Nothing that the spinner wanted. That was the problem.

"Who is she to you? At least tell me that much."

That is the heart of everything, thinks the spinner.

Elke looks exasperated. "Well, you are important to her, too. She's on the lookout for you."

"What? How do you know?"

"She's ordered all the guards and servants to tell her immediately if they should spot you near the castle."

"What did she say? How do you know she talked of me?"

"She spoke of a decrepit man—a spinner. She meant

you." Elke looks him up and down. "She meant the you she saw when she was locked in the cellar. *Decrepit* hardly suits you now, with your strong arms and back."

The spinner swallows with difficulty. "Did she say what she planned to do with me?"

"All she wants is to know if you are nearby."

The spinner nods. "Did you speak to her of me?"

"Of course not. I kept my promise." Elke gives a reproachful *tsk.* "But there was anxiety in her as she spoke. I must know who you are to her. She is queen because of you; of that I have no doubt. All the same, she is my mistress. I risked much when I took you to her in the rooms of straw. I risk much now if I lie to her. I deserve to know why I take these risks."

The spinner hops from the stool and sits beside Elke on the bench. "You take these risks because you care for me."

Elke's eyes go luminous with tears. "Sometimes I wonder if a heart beats within your chest."

The spinner has the urge to caress her cheek, to pull her close, to know her heat. "Promises are to keep."

"Only decent promises. Tell me this, at least. Do you mean good or harm?"

"I love the queen's family," says the spinner, thinking of himself, her true father, and the child in her belly, his true grandchild.

"All right." Elke looks away. "Curiosity grows within me. I wish I understood you. But it is enough that I trust you."

Trust. Who can trust anyone?

Elke walks over and picks up the block of wood by the basket. "What will it be?"

The spinner doesn't answer. She's asked this before, and he's never answered.

Elke lifts a corner of the blanket that covers the basket.

"Stop." The spinner is beside her in a flash. He frees the blanket from her hand. "What I whittle is my business."

"You're so harsh with me." Her eyes glitter with unshed tears. "Do you forget that without me you'd be destitute?"

"No. I never forget."

Elke flushes with frustration. "You expect me to accept every strange habit of yours without question, and you try to shame me when I show the most natural curiosity." She shakes a finger at him. "You infuriate me." She rushes to the corner and picks up the sack of yarns the spinner has spun. "Don't endanger anyone. Anyone." She goes to the door, then she stops and faces him again. "Stay in the woods, out of sight." She leaves.

The spinner stretches his neck forward and rubs the back of it. For the first time, it dawns on him that he will not be able to live with his grandchild here in peace unless Elke consents.

He has several months to figure out how to make that happen. He is afraid he will need them all.

Twenty-seven

WEEKS pass. Months pass. No guard sees the spinner. No servant sees the spinner. Saskia spends hours every day looking from the various windows of the castle.

And when she walks beyond the castle walls, she glances over her shoulder often.

Daily, she conducts the same inquiry with the servants. Have they noticed a slight man? A twisted man? An eager man?

But he doesn't appear. Except in the shadowland of her fears.

Summer turns to fall, turns to winter. Saskia stands at the table fingering the wonderful cloth Elke lays before her. She misses spinning. Winter is easier on her than the other seasons, when the hue of a flower or a leaf makes her whole self ache to create a playful yarn. She mustn't take the chance of creating yarns that recall the spinster she was; she mustn't take the chance of reawakening the king's greed for gold. Saskia's fear always lurks below the surface. Still, seeing the subtle blend of colors in this fine cloth now, feeling its superb evenness hurts. "Did you save my own yarns? Was this made from them?"

Elke smiles. "No, but it's quite lovely, isn't it? A master spinner's work."

"It's a marvel." Saskia yanks the yarn between her hands to test its strength. "I want the baby's wardrobe sewn from cloth woven with this spinner's yarn. Everything, from leggings to blankets."

"I understand, Your Highness."

Saskia grabs a long swatch of cloth and buries her face in it. In this moment she feels safe for the first time since she came to the castle. Everything is going to be all right, after all. The contorted spinner will never come again.

The baby inside her kicks. Always in the same place—her right side, midabdomen. Saskia is sore there. She puts her hand to the spot and pushes lightly. The baby kicks harder. She laughs and wraps the cloth tight around her middle, stealing this respite from fear.

Twenty-eight

THE baby is due in a week. The spinner has not found a way to convince Elke that he should be the one to raise the child. He's only grown more certain that she would be impossible to convince. She talks nonstop about the coming of the child. She's idealized the event. Indeed, the spinner realizes she's in love with the unborn child, with the very idea of the child, in that way that he has noted only in childless women.

But that's all right. He has made plans. He will visit the queen when no one is about. He will take the child and flee. After a year, when everyone has forgotten about him, when the queen has a second child, he can return to this house he's made so perfect. He has already fastened the shutters against the cold of the season. He checks them now; they hold firm. When he leaves, he will bolt the door.

In the meantime, he'll find a home in the center of a distant town in a distant kingdom. That makes sense, anyway. For with a new baby, he'll need the help of women in the town. After all, he doesn't know all the things he should to keep an infant alive. So leaving this home in the woods turns out to be for the best.

All he needs is a horse. He has selected the miller's mare, which he spied from the pine grove behind the mill. The miller is always drunk at night. The horse stands unguarded.

Stealing the mare will be easy.

The spinner has never been a thief before.

Stealing.

Taking the baby isn't stealing, though. After all, this is his grandchild, someone who will share his name.

The spinner strips naked. He runs his hands over the hard muscles of his chest. He still stands twisted over to the right in a crippling distortion. All the exercises in the world couldn't unrumple that leg or straighten his spine after so many years. But he is powerful.

The baby will be called Albrecht if he is a boy, after the spinner's father. Amalie if she is a girl, after the spinner's mother.

He lies down on his bed and pulls up the thick wool blanket. The outline of the bundle he has tied together—all the necessities of life other than food—looms at the foot of his bed. It is ready, too.

Everything will work out for the best.

Names

Twenty-nine

S A S K I A sits before the huge fire-place in the dark wood chair with the carved armrests. She nurses Mathilde. The king stands beside them, rocking backward on his heels as he looks with satisfaction at nothing.

Snow settles thick on the roof and the ground. It gives the sensation of muting the outside world. The crackle of the fire is loud. Mathilde sucks and grunts and makes little smacking noises. Saskia nestles sleepily into the cushions jammed behind her in this chair.

The king strokes Saskia's forehead once, letting his hand lie heavy on her hair for a moment. "I think I'll have pear schnapps. Would you like anything?"

"No, thank you. I'll join you soon."

Elke enters as the king exits. It's as though she's been waiting just beyond the door for this moment. She comes in with both hands extended toward the baby. "Shall I take her from you now?"

Saskia looks down at Mathilde. Her head lolls to the side on Saskia's cradling arm. In her sleep, she smiles ever so slightly. Saskia yields her daughter reluctantly.

Elke kisses Mathilde gently on the top of her head. "Shall I send Bridget to help you?"

"Not yet."

Elke smiles and leaves. Saskia hears her steps on the stairs.

Saskia leans back and looks into the fire. She thought she knew what it meant to love. There was a time when she loved her father, after all. And she loves Dagmar. And when this baby kicked within her, she knew she loved her. But, oh, having the child, holding the child, that's another kind of love entirely. Saskia knows bliss.

She doesn't know what told her—whether it was noise or a shadow—but instantly she grows cold and unutterably sad. The months of looking fruitlessly for the spinner lulled her into false security. Now all the old dread returns, fierce and certain. She turns her head.

He stands there, robust of body. Yet it is definitely him.

Saskia could shout. The king would come running. He'd throw the spinner in prison.

But this spinner has powers.

And knowledge.

His hand cannot be forced; he must be persuaded.

Saskia speaks softly. "I won't give her up."

The spinner leans his crutches against the couch and sits. "You made a promise."

"I know that."

"You owe me your life."

"I don't owe you hers."

"You promised."

Saskia's mouth goes dry. "We have carved chairs and sideboards. Name what you want. We have animals. Strong draft horses. Cows whose milk forms cream a thumb thick at the top of the jug. We have cloth from the most wonderfully spun yarn. I can have the tailor make you a whole wardrobe."

The spinner laughs. "I can spin whatever yarn I want, weave whatever cloth I want."

"Of course." Saskia swallows. Her throat is dry now, too. "And it makes no sense to offer you gold, does it?" She pulls on her fingers. "What do you want?"

"What you promised."

A cry of misery escapes Saskia's lips. "I love her more than life itself. Can't you understand?" Her tears stream.

The spinner sits, his face marble cold; his left hand taps the middle shell of the necklace she gave him. And, yes, on his finger shines that ring, like a ball of gold yarn.

"For the sake of the woman whose necklace that was, whose ring that was, the woman I know you knew—" Saskia rises to her feet as her voice rises. "For her sake, for pity's sake, for the sake of everything good and holy, name your price. Anything. Anything except Mathilde."

"Mathilde." The spinner grimaces. "You named her already."

"Of course."

"A name from nowhere."

Saskia shakes her head in confusion. "Not from nowhere. The king's mother was named Mathilde."

"Names," says the spinner slowly. "Names are important."

Saskia is encouraged by the tremble in the spinner's voice. "Yes."

"Your mother was good at names."

Saskia has no idea what this means. "Yes," she whispers, hopefully.

"She was creative."

Already the skin on Saskia's temples tightens. She doesn't respond.

"And you are creative."

The skin of her scalp tightens now. Fear hums in her ears.

"I see it in your yarns." He points at her. She sinks back into the chair. His finger comes steadily forward, as though it would penetrate her chest, pierce her heart. "All right, child, I'll give you three chances."

Three chances. She strains to understand, strains against the deafening terror.

"For three nights, I came to you and answered your prayers. For three nights, I will come again, starting tomorrow. You will guess my true name. If you guess correctly by the end of the third night, the baby is yours. If you don't, I won't release you from your promise." The spinner stands. He takes his crutches and walks to the courtyard door. He opens it. A gust of freezing wind assails the room. The fire roars.

Thirty

ADOLF."

The spinner smiles. Will she proceed methodically through the alphabet? "No."

"Albrecht."

He laughs as he thinks of his father. "A good name. But no."

"Alois, Alfons, Alex."

"No, no, no."

The queen reads, her voice droning into the night. The list is far from creative; it contains only well-known names. What did she do? Collect the names of all the townsfolk? Ask the names of all their dead as far back as they can remember?

"Wilfried, Wilhelm, Xavier." Her eyelids droop as she speaks the last name.

She is more beautiful in her motherhood than she was in

her girlish virginity. Her fullness becomes her. Even her motherly exhaustion becomes her. "Did you sleep last night, Queen?"

"No." She blinks.

The spinner didn't sleep either. Excitement and anguish alternately pricked him awake. Yet he feels more energetic than ever, as though these ridiculously mundane names fuel his body. He had feared she'd look at him—at his rumpled leg—and she'd remember the stick of a man he was when first she met him—and she'd know his true name, the hateful name her mother gave him. But now he knows that this naive woman doesn't understand what's in a name. She will lose her child, her one love. The spinner has already lost his child and his love. Everybody suffers. It's not the spinner's fault; Saskia brought it on herself. She has no right to make him feel her pain. "Foolish queen."

"Tonight you call me queen." Her eyes shine glassy. "Last night you called me child."

"Titles," he says.

"Or names. Simple names."

"Nothing is simple about a name." He stands. "Surely you can be more resourceful."

She wipes the tears from her cheeks. "So it's an unusual name?"

"Am I an unusual person?" He lowers his chin, and his head sinks a little into his neck. "Doesn't a name reflect the person?"

"Are you trying to help me? Whose side are you on?"

Panic jabs the spinner. She can, indeed, be clever. He takes his crutches and leaves.

Thirty-one

ABRAM."

"A Jewish name?" The spinner smiles. "No."

Did he say that about the name being Jewish just to fool her? Should she skip all the rest of the Jewish names on her list? No, she will not be dissuaded from her path. She'll read every single name. The first day she had the castle guards collect the names of everyone in town. The guard who recited the most names got a roast piglet for his family. Today, the second day, she had them collect every foreign name they'd ever heard—the prize being a cellar of pear schnapps. And she searched her books for more names.

"Aeskeles, Ambrosius, Aristotle, Artus, Attila, August."

"No. No no no no no."

She reads on into the night. When she hits the *L* names, she rests awhile. She has told the king to allow her to sit alone by the fire undisturbed. But now she half wishes that he'd enter. So what if the spinner were to tell him about spinning the straw? It was an ungodly command in the first place. And now there's Mathilde. The king would never put to death the mother of his own daughter. And he has real affection for her now—she believes that. The punishment would be bearable, more bearable than this misery. Maybe she should shout. Maybe she should wake the entire castle.

But the man before her can spin straw into gold. And he gets in here without being seen, night after night, as he did when she was locked in the rooms of straw.

Why does he even bother with this sham right now? He can simply spirit Mathilde away.

Saskia curls around the pain in her heart. She picks up the papers she has let fall to her lap. "Lambert, Lucio . . ." She reads to the very end. ". . . Paolo, Pierre, Pilatus, Ptolemy . . . Zachaus, Zachariah, Zebediah." She drops her head forward.

"You won't find it by asking foreigners."

Saskia jerks her head up. "Will I find it in books?"

"No."

"Where, then?"

The spinner stands and puts his crutches under his arms.

"Don't go. For God's sake, give me a hint."

"Get some sleep, daughter."

The word *daughter* clatters about in her chest vilely.

"Go back to sleep." The king echoes the spinner. He takes Saskia's hand and kneels before her as she sits on the edge of the bed. "The half moons under your eyes darken. You grow wan. Three nights you haven't slept."

Saskia squeezes the king's fingers. She has the urge to tell him everything. After all, he's part of this, him and his unpardonable greed in asking for the impossible. He should take over, rid the world of this mess.

Bridget enters, carrying Mathilde. "All clean and ready for a feeding." She smiles, but her hands move a little too quickly, anxiously. Her eyes, too, show worry. She hands Mathilde to Saskia and arranges the pillows.

Saskia eases into the softness.

"Such a beauty, our daughter." The king smoothes the fine hairs on Mathilde's head and leaves.

Saskia blinks. The word *daughter* has become a puzzle. And now an idea comes to her in a frenzy that makes her heart speed. "Bridget, I need to see the miller."

"Your father?"

"Immediately. Tell Ulrich."

Bridget leaves at a run.

Mathilde nurses greedily, her left arm flopping in the air. Saskia takes that hand within her right one and massages the slender fingers. She lets her head fall toward Mathilde and waits, listless.

"Your father is here, Your Highness."

"Show him in."

Bridget goes out to the hall and returns with the miller.

He stands awkwardly by the bed, his shoulders more stooped than Saskia remembered.

Bridget backs out of the room.

"Hello, daughter." His voice is coarse, as though unaccustomed to being used.

Saskia means to lift her chin and meet his eyes. But she finds herself trembling, fighting off tears.

Father steps closer.

Saskia halts him with a hand gesture.

The miller leans toward Mathilde, and a sloppy gentleness overcomes his features. "My grandchild."

"Her name is Mathilde, and she's in danger."

"Danger?" He looks confused. "Why did you call me here?"

"Maybe you can help me."

"Me?" He hesitates.

"A man came to me when I was locked up with the straw. He helped me."

The miller's face goes slack. "You didn't spin the straw into gold?"

"I don't know magic." Saskia's voice is harsh. But she can't waste time with reprisals. "Mathilde is the only magic I have ever made." She speaks more kindly now, as she shifts Mathilde to the other breast and strokes the baby's back. "I promised this man that I'd give him my firstborn in exchange for spinning the gold. And now he's come to take her."

The miller sinks to a sitting position on the edge of Saskia's bed. "He spins straw into gold, and he wants your child." The skin under the miller's eyes goes blotchy. He practically writhes at his own words. "Who is this man?"

"I don't know. I have to guess his name or he will take Mathilde."

"Describe him to me."

"One leg is withered. He twists to that side; his spine curves sharply. He's a spinner."

A gasp comes from the hall.

"Who is that?" calls Saskia in a panic.

Elke enters.

"You were eavesdropping."

"I couldn't help it, Your Highness. I came to take Mathilde, as always. When I heard a man in your room, I hesitated. Oh, my queen, I know him." Elke's voice is a shrill cry. "I know this spinner."

Saskia clasps Mathilde to her and sits upright. "Tell me his name."

"I don't know it. I've always called him 'my little man.' He's the castle spinner. The blanket you wrap Mathilde in was woven from his yarns."

Saskia clutches Mathilde's blanket in one hand, then releases her fist in horror and watches the fine, soft cloth come open again. The spinner has insinuated himself into their daily lives, covering their very flesh. And he orders that she guess his name or else. The strangeness of the spinner's demand strikes her now. Why is he doing this? Is he totally mad? "He's given me three nights to come up with the name. Two have passed already. Tonight is my last chance."

"It's not hard to find a name," says Elke, wringing her hands.

"I've tried. There's my list." Saskia points to the pile of papers on the table under the window. "I tried German names, then Greek names and Italian names and French names and Hebrew names. I tried every name I could find."

The miller shakes his head. "He claimed none of those names?"

"None."

"Then he goes by a made-up name."

"So you know him, too?" So much is wrong. Saskia feels the world twist.

The miller ignores Saskia's question. He looks at Elke. "Do you know where he lives?"

Tears stream down Elke's face. "Yes," she says at last.

"Send guards to capture him."

"No!" Saskia grabs the miller's arm. "He's magic. Who knows what he'll do."

"He won't do anything. He'll be put to death for threatening the queen."

"I'm afraid." Saskia squeezes the miller's arm and looks at Elke. "Tell the guards where he lives. They must spy and find out his name. But tell them to be careful. They must not let him see them."

Elke's shoulders shake with sobs. She leaves.

Saskia still holds the miller by the arm. "Tell me what you know of him."

The miller shakes his head.

"He called me a strange thing."

"What was that, daughter?"

Saskia stops with the word *daughter* on her tongue. She shivers and falls back on her pillows.

Thirty-Two

T H E spinner checks everything one last time. All is secured. Tonight he leaves this house behind for a year.

He straps his bundle to his back—his clothes and blankets, five wooden animals, a pot and spoon, all tied together with the spinning wheel attached on the outside.

He hikes south, then west. He comes out behind the small stable beside the mill. He leaves the bundle at the base of a pine and hikes back home.

The snow comes up to his ankle, but it is light and kicks away easily. The day warms up nicely. It's almost balmy. It will be an early spring.

He sits on a stump at the edge of his clearing—the stump of that plane tree he tried to fell when he first determined to grow strong again. A rabbit pushes its nose under the snow, not two bodies' length from his foot. He reaches into his back pocket slowly and pulls out the slingshot he whittled. It is not as fine as the large one Hansjakob carved for Thomas on his tenth birthday, but it does the job.

The rabbit stops, waits with one beady eye on him. The spinner secures a stone in the sling. He aims. Shoots. The rabbit is knocked to the ground. It jerks convulsively.

The spinner skins the rabbit, rubs the inside of the pelt with snow, and tucks it into the rope that holds up his pants. Rabbit-hair yarn will make soft, warm leggings for a baby.

He clears snow from the hole for his cooking fires and piles in wood. A blackened skewer runs above, between two forked sticks. He forces the skewer down the throat of the rabbit and out its anus. He lights the fire.

The flames lick at the pink-white flesh. He rotates the skewer often. Dusk comes with a chill. The spinner rubs his arms and moves closer to the fire. He pulls a hunk of bread from the sack over his shoulder and sets it on his baking rock.

The spinner will time his departure to arrive at the castle around midnight—as on the past three nights. By the wee hours of tomorrow, he'll have his granddaughter here—he pats the pouch he's sewn inside his thick shirt, so that the baby can ride safely on his chest. Tears of joy fill his eyes. He hops on one foot round and round the fire, singing:

> Today the meat I roast
> Today the bread I bake
> Tomorrow tomorrow tomorrow
> The queen's baby girl I take
> For she'll never guess her mother's sin

The one who named me Rumpelstiltskin
She'll never guess
So the babe is mine
O joyous night
O rapturous dawn

Thirty-three

SASKIA sits in this chair looking just as she has for the past two nights. But tonight she is armed: The guards brought her his name.

A piteous name.

When he came to her three nights ago, he called it his true name. He said her mother was creative. So Mother must have given him this name. Why would she have been so cruel?

But then, the spinner is cruel. What kind of person would bargain for her firstborn?

The spinner enters at midnight. Saskia knows he comes through the kitchen door, which Elke leaves unlatched for him. Saskia was grateful to learn the secret of his entry. At least that isn't magic.

"Hello, midnight visitor," says Saskia.

The spinner and Saskia look at each other across the room. From this distance, the amount he has changed in the past two years is more remarkable than ever. He is almost handsome. And he looks familiar.

The spinner swings on his crutches. He sits on the floor at her feet. "Speak, Saskia."

She shakes her head. "So tonight it is not *child* or *queen* or *daughter*, but merely my given name? You've called me something different each time you've come."

"And you have no choice but to call me *spinner*. Read from your silly list."

Saskia spreads her hands open on her lap. "I have no list tonight."

"So you give up?" The spinner puts his palms together, as if in prayer. "Where is the child?"

"I don't give up. I'll make my guesses." Saskia leans down toward the spinner. She smells smoke in his clothes. "Why do you want her? What would you do with her?"

The spinner looks into Saskia's eyes. His own are large and clear. "I ive together." His voice is mellow. "I will love her and care for her. Do not worry."

"Do you tell the truth?"

"You keep your promises. I keep mine."

"But do you tell the truth? Are you honest when you speak with Elke?"

"Elke?" The spinner is clearly taken aback at the revelation that Saskia knows of his relationship with Elke. "What point would there be in deceiving her?"

Saskia licks her lips. "Why did you tell Elke that you loved my family?"

The spinner doesn't answer.

"Why did my mother name you?"

The spinner doesn't answer.

Saskia whispers, "Why did you call me *daughter*?"

The spinner stands. "Guess my name or give me the child now."

Something inside Saskia moans with grief. "Broken Wing."

"Is that your guess?"

"One of them."

"No."

"Broken Leg."

"It isn't broken. No."

"Broken Heart."

"You're wasting our time."

"Is your name . . ." Saskia's voice sounds faint, even to herself. Suddenly she knows she is about to destroy him, this man who wants to love and live with her child. "Is your name, perhaps, Rumpelstiltskin?"

The spinner's face crumbles as Saskia's heart crumbles. "You couldn't know. You couldn't have guessed on your own." He pulls his hair. "Devils speak through your mouth." He stomps his feet. His rumpled leg flies uncontrollably, as though pedaling the floor—*thump thump thump.* He grabs at the empty air. "Dust devils. My devils." His leg pounds relentlessly with unnatural force. It breaks through the floor. The spinner tries to pull himself free, but he is caught. He is a prisoner of that leg. That leg that even now pumps inside the hole and shakes him to the top of his head. He yanks away with so much force, he rips asunder. He hops to the courtyard doors, a river of blood flowing from his groin. He throws them open with a scream that shatters glass. He disappears into the night, his rumpled leg still pumping in the hole. Pumping, pumping.

Saskia drops to her knees. Blood and tears and milk merge. Everything twists. Like that leg.

That leg that goes still, at last.